ST DUM

D0297136

C 03 0309223

THE RED GLOVES
AND OTHER STORIES

CATHERINE FISHER

Firefly

First published in 2021
by Firefly Press
25 Gabalfa Road, Llandaff North, Cardiff, CF14 2JJ
www.fireflypress.co.uk

Text copyright © Catherine Fisher 2021

A CIP catalogue record of this book is
available from the British Library.

Print ISBN 9781913102685
ebook ISBN 9781913102692

This book has been published with the support
of the Books Council of Wales.

Typeset by Elaine Sharples

Printed and bound by CPI Group (UK) Ltd,
Croydon, Surrey, CRO 4YY

CONTENTS

INTRODUCTION

This book contains nine stories that were written over many years. Some of them have been published in other collections or anthologies, others are fairly new and have not appeared before.

Short stories are fascinating to write; in them the writer can focus on single actions or brief moments that might be lost in a novel. However at least two stories here, or their events in them, were reworked into novels at a later date, and it's surprising how the same situation can be completely changed and re-imagined in a new and interesting way.

'The Silver Road' came from an idea about two brothers sharing the same dream. As I wrote it I became more aware of how dangerous and alluring a dream could be, and the relationship between the boys also became clearer. I like the end of this story, with its suggestions of other strange worlds out there to explore. 'The Red Gloves' was great fun to write, though I hope I wasn't too unfair to poor Katy. Again, the magical element of the story was my first idea, and as I wrote it the events made the two girls and the awkward nature of their friendship become clearer.

'The Hare' was written for a short-story competition. The adjudicator was the great Jenny Nimmo, author of *The Snow Spider*, so it was thrilling to receive praise from a writer I very much admire. Most of these stories are set in Wales, this one at Tintern in the Wye valley, a place I know well, and it uses themes from the Taliesin legend. And I was lucky enough to win the competition with it!

I have always found changing rooms strange and rather spooky places. So 'The Changing Room' story came into my mind one day when I was in one – probably with one sock on and one sock off. I like the idea of swapping identities, and again it reworks part of an old legend, from the First Branch of the Mabinogi. 'Sgilti Lightfoot' is a story based in the crazy and magical world of Arthur's court, which I really like. In one of those old tales there is a list of Arthur's famous men, who have all sorts of powers; Sgilti is one, so light he can run on the top of grass blades without breaking them. I stole him and wrote a story about him.

Mirrors are spooky too. There always seems to be something else in them, just behind you. In 'The Mirror', the bird Daniel sees emerging through the glass might be real or might be something inside him that needs to come out and only the mirror can make that happen.

'Nettle' is a version of an old English folktale, called Yallery Brown. In the original version – you should read it! – Yallery Brown is very scary, and comes out as the winner, but here I wanted Nettle to be so mysterious that you might wonder if he even exists or if he is an aspect of Nia herself.

The final two stories in the book are the ones that have themes that became novels. 'Not Such a Bad Thing' is based on something that really happened (but not to me!) I used the situation again in my novel *Crystabel*.

And in 'The Ghost in the Rain' I wanted to create a classic Victorian ghost story with a girl and a boy and an old house and a deep well, and it was only when I was preparing it for this volume that I realised it has a setting in common with my novel *The Clockwork Crow*, even though it was written long before that book, and is very different. Obviously those things were deep in my mind waiting to come back out and be re-created, all that time.

I hope you enjoy the stories.

Catherine Fisher

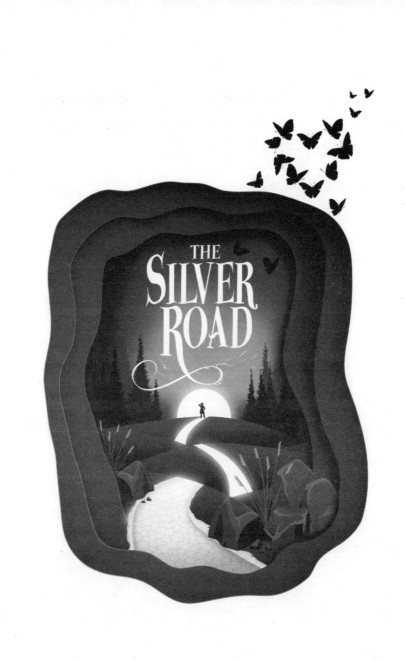

THE SILVER ROAD

 Tom opened his eyes.

He lay still for another minute, staring up at the ceiling, listening to the increasingly restless sounds from the other bed. Finally he heaved the bedclothes aside and got up. Weariness surged over him as he crossed the room.

Simon was asleep, curled under the blue quilt, twitching and muttering. Tom looked at the tiny gleaming hands of the clock. Quarter to three. Bang on time.

He bent over and took a fold of warm pyjama sleeve between finger and thumb. 'Si! Simon. Wake up.'

The movement stopped, with one small shudder. Simon lay still, facing the wall.

'Are you awake?' Tom whispered.

'Yes.'

Tom went for his dressing gown, hanging on the

back of the door. He paused, listening, but there was no sound from his mother's bedroom. He dragged the dressing gown on, glad of its warmth, then came and sat on Simon's bed, pulling the quilt over his cold feet.

'Do you want the light on?'

'Yes.'

When the lamp clicked on, a soft yellow glow showed them the familiar room: its huddle of clothes on the window seat, the pictures of ships, the cloud of mobiles that hung and drifted from the ceiling – Simon's flock of carved, multicoloured birds.

Simon lay silent for a moment, then turned over and sat up against the pillow, pushing the long fair hair out of his eyes. He looked very tired. Tom nudged the bedclothes. 'Keep warm. Did you manage to touch the road this time?'

Simon shrugged. 'The road was the same – it always is. Smooth and silver and cold underfoot. I remembered to touch it, like you said, but I'm still not sure what it's made of.' He yawned and rubbed one eye. 'You'd better get the book.'

Tom bent down, opened the cupboard and pulled

out an old notebook full of half-empty pages. He turned them, noting the date of each entry, sometimes in his neat round writing, ragged with sleeplessness, sometimes in Simon's spiky scrawl. They had written in it every night for two months.

He took a pen out of the drawer and wrote *Thursday 23rd May 2.45am* and then looked up at his stepbrother. 'OK. Go ahead.'

'I walked along the road,' Simon said quietly, 'towards the wood. I was just where I had been last night. The road went downhill. This time it was raining – big heavy spots. I soon got wet.'

Still writing, Tom said, 'Were those birds there?'

'No. There was just cloud: grey and low. I walked quickly and even ran a bit but it seemed to take ages to get anywhere – it always does. The moon came up, on my right. The wood got closer. There was no sound but the rain.'

'What was on each side of the road?' Tom asked. A sound in the other bedroom made them stop and listen, but after a while Simon whispered, 'The same. Hillsides of grass and bushes. Blackthorn, rowan, hawthorn. A few trees.'

Tom jotted it down quickly.

9

'It seemed to take me about an hour,' Simon went on, winding a corner of the sheet around his finger, 'till I got to the wood. It was very dark in there; the road ran straight through the trees, I could see it shining in the dimness. I thought I'd have to go on, but I could hear water trickling and I wanted to go and see where it was – I was very thirsty all of a sudden. Then I saw a stream – like the others a few nights ago. It was bubbling up and running through the grass not far from the road, over some stones. It was very clear.'

He stared thoughtfully at the drifting mobiles. In the dim light their shadows wandered the ceiling. Outside, a lorry strained up the hill and rattled into the distance.

'Go on,' Tom said. 'What happened?'

'I really wanted a drink. I walked right to the edge of the road.' He sat up suddenly and stared at Tom. 'But I had that feeling! Exactly the same … my heart pounding and my hands all sweaty. I knew if I stepped off the road, Tom, I was lost! Just lost.'

Tom watched him for a moment. He was almost too tired to think. They both were. He even felt a

10

bitter twinge of envy. Why did he never dream of this place?

Simon lay back. 'And that's it. I woke up. Maybe just in time.'

There was silence in the room. Tom finished writing and glanced back over the pages. 'We're still no nearer knowing what causes it, or what to do.'

'I just want it to stop.'

They both did. At first it had been a joke, something to laugh about, but now it was a worry: a secret, growing fear. Now they only spoke about the dream to each other, and Tom often caught himself puzzling about it, at meals, on the bus, in lessons. He found it hard to concentrate on anything else anymore. Simon was good at art, he played the violin, everyone said he was the imaginative one, but this wasn't right. It wasn't normal.

He cleared the worried look from his face. 'It'll go.'

'It had better,' Simon said simply, 'because how long can we go without sleeping properly? And I know there's something waiting for me, Tom.

Someone at the end of that road.' He closed his eyes and rolled over. 'It's not just a dream. It's real.'

Tom closed the book. His hands were cold. After a moment he put the lamp out.

✱✱✱

'The same dream?' Ieuan Lewis said, sitting on the table. 'A continuous dream?'

'Night after night.' Tom tossed his half-eaten sandwich into the metal bin marked ADRAN GELF and stared out of the window at the pupils of Ysgol Llanharan running out of the rain. 'And he says it's so real. He's really there, and he can remember it, not like ordinary dreams. Even the weather is real.'

The bell silenced him; its electric scream made them both jump slightly, though they'd been expecting it. When it stopped, Ieuan twisted a strand of his hair between a cobalt thumb and a yellow-splashed finger. 'That explains something. I always thought Simon had talent but... Come and look at this.'

Ieuan was the art teacher. He was also Tom's first

cousin, and not one of his teachers, which made things easy between them. Now he rummaged among a pile of folders and pulled one out with *Simon Owen Jones* scrawled across it in pen. He took a painting out of it that Tom stared at in astonishment.

The silver road ran between boulders on a high hillside. A stream glinted beside it. On each side, in Simon's intricate brushwork, were gorse bushes, bracken, high banks of hawthorn, bright bluebells. Butterflies danced in the pale sky. The empty road ran down to a distant wood, and beyond it the horizon was a blue wash, with a suggestion of far misty hills, blurring into the white paper.

'I thought it was a real place,' Ieuan said. 'I asked him about it, but he was a bit evasive. This explains why.'

Tom shook his head. 'This was from last week. He's right down to that wood now. Tonight he'll be in among the trees. Where is it all leading to?'

Ieuan fingered the painting. A dozen Year Nines crashed through the double doors outside and roared down the corridor like a tide. When the noise had passed, he said, 'You get on all right with him, don't you? When your parents got married, I think they were a bit worried about whether you would.'

Tom shrugged. 'It was strange at first. Especially sharing a room. We had a few big arguments, even a fight once. But not for ages.' He smiled. 'Perhaps this dream's had one good result.'

'You must be tired though.'

Tom nodded.

'Well, it's not right. He should see someone. A doctor. Does his father know? Or Kate?'

'Neither.' Tom thought of his mother and Rhys Jones, imagined, in a brief vivid moment, their astonishment. 'After all, what's a dream, love?' his mother would say. 'It can't hurt you. Don't worry about it.'

'Beats me,' Ieuan said. 'But you really ought to get him to see someone. If it goes on it could affect his health. Yours too.'

∗∗∗

Too right, Tom thought on the way home, watching Simon's wan reflection in the bus window. As they got off by the pub and began the long trudge up the hill, he said, 'Maybe it won't come tonight.'

'Maybe.'

They walked in silence between the grey stone walls. Once, Simon stumbled, the long fringe of hair swinging into his eyes. Angrily, he kicked a stone out of the way. 'Sometimes I'm almost scared to go to sleep.'

'That's daft.'

'You don't know. It doesn't happen to you.' He stopped and looked across the valley, at the small terraces of houses and the green tumble of trees that marked the river. 'It's getting worse, Tom, the further I go. But I daren't step off the road.'

'It's just a dream,' Tom growled, hating himself.

And rain began to fall on them, a stinging downpour.

✶✶✶

The bedroom was dark and still; Tom drifted up to it through veils of fatigue, hauling himself stupidly to the surface. Then he lay there, half asleep. There had been some sound, something; he dragged it

15

back to his memory – a cry, a gasp. He opened his eyes and struggled up onto one elbow.

Simon was a dark huddled shape in the corner of his bed, completely still. Tom closed his eyes and listened to the slow, regular breathing. Then sleep closed over him, like a dark sea.

✷✷✷

'Not at the table,' his mother said, whisking his phone away and putting down the box of cereal. She went out into the hall and they heard her calling, 'Simon! It's almost eight!'

Rhys Jones turned the newspaper over. 'Glamorgan are playing Saturday. We'll go, if you like?'

Tom shrugged. He knew Simon hated cricket. 'I don't mind.'

'I see they've recalled Lloyd. Now there's a mistake.'

But Tom, sprinkling sugar, was listening to his mother upstairs.

'Rhys,' she called. 'Come here, quick.' Her voice sounded strange.

His stepfather hurried out. Tom ate a few

spoonfuls but the voices upstairs, urgent and insistent, burrowed into his mind. He went out into the hall; his mother had her phone out.

'What's wrong?'

She flung him a quick, distant look. 'It's Simon… Hello?… Yes! Ambulance please…'

Shock seemed to drain Tom of all thought. He raced upstairs and into the bedroom.

Simon's father turned a white face to him. 'He won't wake up! I can't wake him!'

Simon lay on his side, head on one arm. He breathed evenly, his face pale but quiet. Tom shook him and called him, but nothing happened. His mother ran in behind him. 'They're coming,' she said.

She went round and brushed Simon's hair from his forehead. 'Simon, love,' she whispered. 'Wake up.'

When the ambulance men came, Tom was ushered out. Downstairs, he fed the cat, his mind numb. There were voices, doors banging, the paramedic running upstairs, his stepfather's deep, bewildered questions. He forced himself to go out into the hall. His mother ran down and grabbed his arm. 'We're going to the hospital. Will you stay here?'

He nodded miserably.

'You should go to school.'

'How can I?'

'All right. I'll phone. Don't worry.' She tugged her coat on and kissed him briefly. 'Don't worry. It might be nothing. I'll phone.'

When they were gone, the house was silent. He sat at the bottom of the stairs for a long time, listening to the silence. Finally he got up, washed the dishes and made the beds. It would be all right. Simon was just very tired. He would wake up and find himself in the hospital. Tom imagined the scene even down to the words. Simon would ask for something to drink. He'd be surprised. Rhys would call him 'son' and joke with the nurses. Everyone would be tearful with relief.

Minute by minute, the morning dragged on, the sun altering the shadows on the mountain. He wandered from room to room, picking things up, putting them down, reading the paper, scuffing up weeds in the garden.

At ten past twelve his phone rang. His mother said, 'There's no change. He hasn't even moved.'

'What do they think it is?'

'They're not sure. Doing tests. You know, all sorts of things.'

'How's Rhys?'

She sighed. 'Beside himself, quietly.'

'Can I come down?'

There was a muffled call from someone in the background. She said, 'Come this afternoon. Get something to eat.'

He made some sandwiches and threw most of them away, then ran down the lane to the bus stop. It was almost an hour to the town; the bus dawdled down the valley, between the steep green slopes of forestry. In the end he wanted to get out and run and run.

The hospital was a white maze of corridors and signs and rooms. They let him see Simon briefly; he looked so normal, just asleep, as if he would wake any minute. As Tom stood there, he heard his mother rattling on nervously to the nurse in the corridor, '...stepbrothers ... we thought when we married ... but after all they get on extremely well,

19

better than we do...' Then her strange, gasping laugh.

At half past six they made him go home. 'I'll have to stay,' his mother said. 'Will you be all right by yourself? Shall I phone Ieuan?'

He shook his head. 'I'll manage.'

Climbing the lane to the house he paused and leaned on a gate, watching the dusk descend slowly on the houses and the mountain. Simon was lost somewhere, in that other country. The doctors had talked about coma and cataleptic states, but Tom knew what had happened. Simon had stepped off the road. And only he knew anything about it.

At eight o'clock he went around and locked the house up, then went upstairs to the bedroom. Deliberately he took a pair of Simon's clean pyjamas from a drawer and put them on. Then he turned back the corner of the blue quilt and climbed into Simon's bed. It was a brass one, brought from Simon's old house. It felt hard, and a little tall.

He switched the light out and lay back. Now for the hardest part. He had to go to sleep.

The room was quiet; he could hear the bleat of

sheep from the fields at Ty'r Nant. The bird-mobiles drifted their dim wings under the ceiling, turning and banking, wing-tip to wing-tip with their shadows.

Darkness fell on him. And sometime later, he fell asleep.

***

He was standing on the silver road. It shone, like Simon had said, but he was astonished at its brightness in the full moonlight. It was like standing on the metal bar of a brooch. The land on each side was dark, but he could smell grass and soil and some familiar, salty tang. He looked around.

'Simon?'

The wood was just ahead of him; he could have touched the nearest tree trunk. Cautiously, he walked forward.

The road glinted between wet leaves and the boles of trees. It ran downhill through the wood, often twisting back on itself, narrowing to a thread sometimes between rocks where great ferns sprouted; sometimes it was so steep that he had to hold on to branches and lower himself carefully.

At the bottom of one steep part he stopped for breath. The night was quiet around him, a murmur of leaves and rustles, the far squeak of bats.

'Simon!' he called. 'It's Tom!'

'*Tom*! Down here!'

The voice came from in front of him, where the path twisted sharply; beside it a sheer drop fell into darkness. Tom took a step, and saw. Simon was a little way down, clinging to a log that seemed to have slithered down with him. If he moved, the whole thing might crash down.

Tom scrambled to the very edge of the road and stopped. He dared not leave it. If he did, neither of them might ever wake up again.

He knelt down. 'Are you all right?'

'Cuts, that's all. But there's nothing to hold on to.'

Tom stretched out, gripping a beech trunk with his other hand, but his fingers slid on the smooth bole. 'Wait. This is no good.' He looked round.

Simon watched him. 'Don't leave the path.'

'I won't.'

He lay down, coiling one foot under a root.

Then he slithered forwards carefully, until he was hanging well over the edge of the road, head downwards. His straining fingers touched Simon's sleeve; he grabbed tight, slid down to the wrist, then the hand. Simon edged nearer; a shower of leaves and soil collapsed and crashed far below.

'Now!' Tom gasped, both hands gripping tight. 'Let go!'

Simon dug his toes in and made a leap upwards; the sudden weight almost dragged Tom off the road but he hung on, gritting his teeth against the pain in his foot. There was a moment of scrambling and squirming then, slowly, between breaths, he pulled his stepbrother up the shifting bank and over, onto the shining road.

They crouched, aching, breathless.

Finally Simon said, 'You got here then.'

'Yes. And now I'm here, I want to see where this road ends.' Tom scrambled up. 'Don't you?'

Simon laughed sourly. But he stood up.

Around the next turn of the road, they found the end of the wood, and they saw with a shock of delight that the sea was before them, black and

23

shining, the moon's track glinting across it. They could see the silver road spilling itself down the hillside, across the shingle, and right into the water that spread and ebbed over it.

'It goes into the sea!' Tom muttered.

'Yes. But look out there.'

Far out, dim against the dark sky, was an island. Small lights glinted on it.

'Let's go down.'

Quickly they ran to the sea's edge, into the noise of the waves, crashing and sucking and rolling the shingle of the beach. Spreading fans of water ran over their bare feet.

Tom jerked back. 'It's cold!'

Bobbing in the tide, with no rope to hold it there, was a small boat, half invisible in the darkness. Two oars lay in the bottom; it seemed to have been left there for them.

Far out in the night, the lights on the island gleamed blue and green.

'Will you go?' Tom said, after a long moment.

Simon laughed briefly, then shook his head. 'I'd like to. I mean, what's out there? How far can anyone go, into his imagination? But I know this,

Tom, that if we did we'd never get back. Only the road is safe.'

Tom nodded. 'Do you think we'll be coming here again?'

'I doubt it.' As he spoke, Simon seemed to get fainter. He laughed again. 'See you later, Tom. I think someone's waking me up…'

When he was alone on the road, Tom took one last look at the island. 'Maybe one day,' he said, quietly. Then he turned in surprise, hearing the sound that had begun in the air, a high, familiar, insistent call, repeated over and over.

✷✷✷

When he opened his eyes he was in bed, and his phone was ringing. For a second he lay there, watching the painted birds drift against the ceiling. Then he sat up lazily and grinned.

He knew already what his mother would have to say.

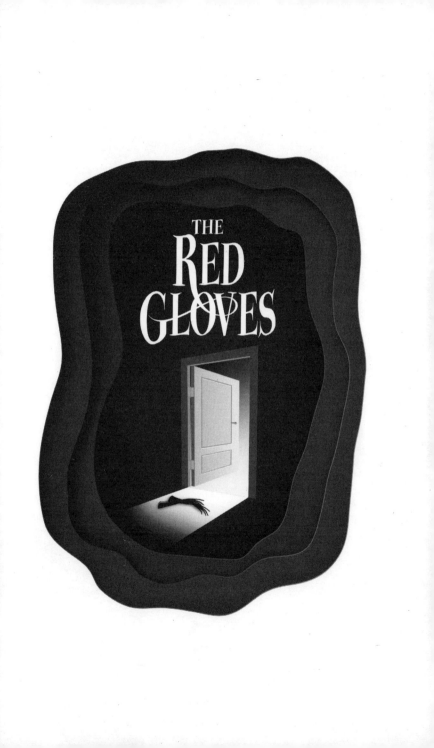

THE RED GLOVES

2

Monday 16th April

They were red and they only cost a pound.

When I picked them up they felt silky. I pulled the left one on, though the woman behind the stall gave me a sharp look.

It fitted perfectly. I flexed my suddenly elegant fingers. The gloves were old, maybe Victorian and long, right up to the elbow, the sort ladies wore with evening dresses at balls and parties.

'Only a pound,' the woman said. She wore a thick coat and a money pocket strapped like an apron around her waist.

'I don't know,' I muttered, but my hand was already pulling money out of my pocket – all I had left since I'd paid Jamie what I owed him.

The pound coin glinted in the slim red fingers. They passed it over to her, then picked up the other glove, daintily, before I'd even realised.

Annoyed with myself, I pulled the glove off. It clung to my fingers and turned itself inside out, all the hairs on my arm standing up. Static. Maybe they weren't silk after all.

I rolled them up and went to look for Mam.

She was at Thomas' Veg and her basket was full. Katy's not coming till tomorrow and you'd think it was the Queen. I've had to clean the spare bedroom twice. I'm getting to think it wasn't worth the bother of inviting her to stay.

I've put the gloves in my drawer, with the other junk. I can't believe I wasted a pound on them.

*Thursday, 17*th

Katy was waiting on the platform. She looks a lot taller, and her hair has grown; it's long now and shinily blonde. She's got new jeans too. I'd forgotten how pretty she was.

In the car coming home she talked about London and her school and her dogs, on and on, and the rest of us could hardly get a word in. Dad flicked me a wink in the driving mirror. I just glared out of the window.

It's strange, but when you don't see someone for

ages you change them in your mind, make them nicer, forget all the little things that irritated you. It made me realise I'd only known her for a fortnight on holiday, and then texts and stuff. It made me realise I didn't really know her at all.

Lunchtime

Something a bit odd has happened. Someone's been messing around in my room. Katy was unpacking; I came in to get her some hangers and my top drawer was open. When I looked in, I saw that all my rings, even the silver one from Nan, were threaded on the fingers of the red gloves.

I marched downstairs and yelled at Jamie.

'Not me. Honest,' he said. He seemed surprised, and didn't laugh or anything.

So who else?

I couldn't believe Katy would be that nosy. When I told her about it, she just smiled. Anyway, this afternoon we're going up to the farm to ride. Brilliant!

5pm

What a day this is turning out to be.

First, she wouldn't come riding. She'd told me in

Spain how good she was, but when I said where we were going she'd looked at me as if I was from Mars. 'I can't!' she wailed. 'I haven't got my hat, or jacket, or anything!'

I told her they'd lend her a hat but she still wouldn't. In the end I went by myself and she stayed sunbathing in the garden. 'Bad manners,' Dad said. 'You should look after your guest, maybe she's just missing home.' But I was annoyed. Farm ponies weren't good enough, by the look of it. And the way she looked round our house when she arrived!

Then when I got back I came up here to change, and stood in the doorway and screeched. The cat had got in. He was sitting on the windowsill washing, and all the things on my desk had been knocked over and all the pens out of my pencil case: my new colours tipped out.

'Get out!' I yelled.

The cat just looked. He rules this place.

Shoving everything back, I shook my sketchbook out from underneath the mess. It was open and there were marks all over the white page, strange, loose writing, as if someone was learning or had nothing to rest on.

WE DON'T LIKE IT HERE.

It was done in pink; the pastel lay there, one soft corner crumbled. I picked it up and put it back, thoughtfully, into the grey sponge slot of its box. Cats don't write. And Jamie had been out.

It was only then, looking in the drawer, that I saw the smudges on the gloves. The left forefinger and thumb. The same pink.

Whoever did the writing wore my gloves.

This is stupid.

Wednesday 18th

I'll just have to come out with it and ask her. But she'll only say it wasn't her. Like the knocking.

It woke me at about one o'clock this morning; I could see the time on my bedside clock. For a moment I lay there, I may even have gone back to sleep, but when it started again my eyes shot open.

Knock. Knock.

It was somewhere in the room. Very quiet, There were scuffles too, oddly muffled, and then again:

Knock. Knock.

I sat up, rigid.

It was coming from across the room; the spare bedroom was on the other side of that wall. My wardrobe and desk were black shapes in the dimness.

'Who's there?' I hissed.

It stopped, instantly.

I swung my legs out and waited, heart pounding. Nothing, except for one tiny scrape.

I must have sat in the dark for half an hour, frozen, listening so intently I could hear all the sounds in the house, even the fridge downstairs and the soft snoring from Dad's bedroom.

At last I realised I was stiff and cold; huddling back under the duvet I lay there till my feet got warm and I must have fallen asleep like that, still listening.

This morning, at breakfast, I asked her.

'Did you knock on the wall in the night?'

Katy looked at me. 'Me? I thought it was you.'

I just stared. She opened her eyes wider. 'Is this house haunted?'

'No, of course it isn't.' I shook my head. 'It must have been … mice.'

That scared her. 'Oh, yuk. I hate mice.'

'Why don't you take Katy out for a walk?' Dad said, coming in with the bacon. 'Up to Druid's Ring, maybe.'

The Ring was a stone circle, my special place. I'd been looking forward all winter to showing it to Katy, but looking at her now, I felt uneasy. I suddenly saw it as she would see it, cold and bleak, just the moors and the stones, with no magic.

Dad was smiling at her. 'Would you like that?'

She nodded, reluctantly, but afterwards she said, 'When are we going into town?'

'Town? What for?'

'Just to buy things. Hang around the shops.'

'You've just come from London,' I muttered. 'We don't have shops like you're used to!' Thinking of her face when she saw Aberglas High Street made me grin.

After that, upstairs, getting my boots on, I found the second note. Blue crayon this time.

WE'RE NOT HAPPY. THIS IS NOT THE SORT OF HOUSE WE EXPECTED. IT'S TOO POKY AND SHABBY. WE ARE USED TO SOMETHING BETTER.

I gaped, then crushed it into my pocket, savagely. What was going on? I'll ask her straight out, now, when we get to the top of the hill.

Teatime
'I'm me, not we,' she said, reading the paper. 'Of course I didn't write it.' But she was laughing, so I just don't know.

She was bored on Druid's Ring. Once she even looked at her watch. When we came back I noticed how she looked around, and all of a sudden I wished the carpet wasn't so grubby and we had nicer wallpaper and things. I was annoyed she made me think like that. I'd never thought about it before.

Later

DIDN'T YOU GET OUR MESSAGE? IF WE ARE NOT TAKEN SOMEWHERE MORE BEFITTING OUR STATUS WE WILL MAKE THINGS VERY UNPLEASANT FOR YOU.

It was lying on the bathroom floor, and all around it were labels, receipts, notes, even clean tissues, all torn into hundreds of tiny white scraps. I stared down at the mess.

'Well?' Mam said icily.

'It wasn't me.'

Katy came in behind me. I caught her face in the mirror as she saw everything. 'What's going on?'

'Nothing.' Smoothly, Mam snatched the dustpan and swept, her lips tight. 'Nothing at all. Now, you come on in.'

Katy looked at me and shrugged, but I marched into my bedroom and, after a second, pulled open the drawer.

The gloves lay hand in hand. Holding hands.

They looked smug somehow; their creases smiled.

I pulled them out and put them on, held up my red fingers and admired them. Whose gloves had they been; what had the hands inside them done, all those years ago?

They felt silky and cool, made me feel different, older, colder, cruel. Almost without wanting to, I picked up a photo of Katy and me on holiday, on the

37

beach. We were grinning and waving, but before I knew it the red fingers had torn the photo in two, the white, jagged edge straight down Katy's face.

I dropped it, horrified.

Then I peeled off the gloves and crammed them into the drawer.

Sulky, they curled together.

I locked the drawer and jammed the key in my pocket.

10.00pm

We've just had a row. She said all sorts of hateful things. That I wasn't like she remembered! ME! I feel hot and furious and I can't sleep; I'm just sitting up here in bed and I'll break this pencil if I hold it any tighter.

She's not the same person. She won't go swimming, or ride, or walk; all she wants to do is shop! And she makes comments under her breath about Dad's cooking, and our house, and she sulks and looks bored.

I could strangle her!

I wish she'd go home!

Thursday. Can't remember date.

I'm scared.

I woke up an hour ago with the sun coming in through the windows and I turned over, sleepily.

When I saw the gloves, I went rigid. They were lying on the carpet in the middle of the room, stretched out, one nearer the bed than the other. I sat up, shivering, my skin prickling. I had the sudden horrible idea that they'd been crawling. Crawling towards the bed.

I leapt out frightened, circled round them, and went to the drawer. The lock was broken. It hung open.

For a moment, I thought of going to get Jamie – he was up, I could hear him whistling in the bathroom – but then I thought, no. It was stupid; he'd just laugh.

Carefully, I went back to the gloves. I knelt down, my face close to them.

They twitched.

I jerked back with a gasp. Then angrily I swept them up, holding them so tight they were a crumpled ball. I looked round. I should get rid of them. But they were gloves. Just gloves. It was pathetic.

39

In the end I tied them in a knot, marched into the spare bedroom and flung them in the chest there, an old iron chest, with a thick padlock. As I twisted the key round, Katy sat up in bed. I was so shaky I'd even forgotten she was there.

'What's that?' she asked, coldly.

'Mind your own business.' I stood up. 'Breakfast's ready. If you can bring yourself to eat it.'

She pouted, settling back on the pillow. 'You're horrible, Sarah. You're spoiling everything.'

'*I'm* spoiling it?' I scowled down at her, so furious that there was nothing I could say. I just got out.

Friday

We spent all day not talking.

Dad took us to some castles and a pub for lunch and she was nice as pie to him, but we hardly said a word. When we got back, she was on her phone for an hour. Then she said she was tired and went up to bed early.

While she was in the shower, I crept in and checked the lock of the chest – it was tight. The key was in my room. Sitting on my own bed, I thought about the gloves. I should burn them. That was what you did with evil things; it was no good selling them, or giving them away, because someone else would have the same trouble all over again.

In the morning, I'd do it!

I was tired, and I suppose I fell asleep without knowing it. I'd been reading, and the book fell off the bed in the night; the thump woke me.

I opened my eyes, then closed them, and lay still.

Absolutely still.

In that glimpse, I had seen someone in the room, a dark small figure, leaning over my desk. Icy with sweat, I opened my eyes a slit.

Nothing.

The room was black and starlit, the door ajar.

Ajar!

I sat bolt upright. I distinctly remembered shutting the door last night.

I forgot about being scared. I jumped out of bed and went straight to the desk and scrabbled hurriedly through the drawer. The key was gone! The key to the iron chest!

41

Instantly, I knew what she was doing. I ran out on the landing and grabbed her door handle, just in time to feel the bolt click across it. I shook it, ferociously. 'Katy!' I hissed. '*Katy!*'

There was silence. Then: 'Go away, Sarah.'

'Don't open it! Listen! *Don't open the chest!*'

When she spoke next, her voice was further from the keyhole. 'Why shouldn't I? You're always keeping secrets from me.'

I slammed my hands against the door in a squirm of rage. 'Because … it's dangerous!'

'Don't be silly,' she muttered.

There was a click and a creak; the lid opening. I tugged desperately at the door, terrified of waking the others. Or should I just scream and scream till they all came?

'It's only a pair of gloves!' Her voice was bitter with disappointment.

'I could have told you that!'

'Then what's the big secr—?' She gasped. The lid of the chest fell with a clang.

'Katy?' I yelled. 'KATY!'

Choking, breathless rasps of noise.

I threw myself against the door and felt it give,

then flung harder, the old bolt splintering the soft wood. Inside, something fell over, kicked, scrabbled. There was a strangled screech.

My mother called, 'Is that you, Sarah?'

I gave one almighty shove and the door gave way so abruptly that I fell headlong into the room. In the dark, I saw her tearing at the hands around her neck, tugging and gasping, and then I flicked on the light and she was coughing, on her knees over the chest, and the red gloves were on the floor, squirming and wriggling.

I wanted to stamp on them hard. Instead I picked them up and flung them back in the chest. We stared at each other, breathless.

Astonished.

4.00pm
She's gone.

At the station we had to wait a few minutes. Dad went back to the car.

'I'm sorry,' she said, really stiffly. 'I suppose I was a bit of a pain.'

I looked away down the platform. 'So was I.'

'It was all so different in Spain. Remember the

diving board at the pool in the hotel, and that time you knocked the glass off the waiter's tray?'

We giggled. For a moment we were back there, again, those other people. Then I said, 'You could come another time.'

'Or you could come to London.'

I nodded, watching the train come in. We both knew I wouldn't go.

I waved, on and on, until the train went round the bend and there was no one left on the platform. Then I dawdled out. Dad was waiting by the car. 'Cheer up,' he said. But I don't think he knew what I was upset about.

When I got home, I ran upstairs and stood in the doorway of the spare room, aghast. The bed was made, and the chest was open.

I hurtled downstairs.

'You sound like a herd of elephants,' my mother said.

'The gloves!' I gasped. 'Where are they?'

'What gloves?'

'Red ones. They were in the chest!'

She frowned. 'Oh. All that stuff was for the charity shop. Mrs Owen came for it.'

44

I stared at her until she said, 'I don't remember you having red gloves.'

'No.' At the door, I turned. 'Where's the shop?'

'She runs a few. In different towns. I don't know where they'll end up.'

I tugged my hair. They wouldn't like that, not a charity shop. I felt sorry for whoever got them next.

Still, I felt so relieved they'd gone.

Mam grinned. 'Katy get her train all right?'

'Mm.'

She nodded. 'Pity about you two. I always thought you were two of a pair.'

I poured a glass of orange juice from the fridge and drank it.

'So did I,' I said. 'So did I.'

THE HARE

3

 'I'm sure they can arrest us for this.' Owen shoved his hands in his pockets and kicked at the muddy bank. 'Any archaeologist would be annoyed. This is some sort of barrow.'

'Was. Caer Ceridwen, it was called, but it was ploughed out years ago. The stuff is all in the museum in Cardiff.' His uncle's hands were rough with the metal detector; he swept it like a scythe, a long, low cut through the air. It beeped suddenly.

'There!' Jack Hughes stubbed his boot in the furrow. 'Try there.'

Reluctantly, Owen crouched again, out of the wind that whistled up through the trees and the black spines of the hedgerow. The soil was frozen on top, but under that it was still soft, like fudge. He sliced the trowel through it. The top of a beer can glinted.

His uncle swore briefly. 'Well, that's it. It's not here.'

He turned his back on the wind, pulled a handful of grubby items out of his pocket, and picked mud off them. 'Let's see what we've got. An old shilling. A nail. A lump of lead.'

'Could be a fishing weight,' Owen suggested.

His uncle weighed it in his hand. 'Could be. But then how did it get up here? Must be a story to that… Two tin can pulls. A bolt – from a tractor, I should think. And this.'

The last was a thin disc about the size of a saucer, covered with a blue-white powder that came off on his hands. He examined it. 'Could be anything. Looks old.'

Owen frowned. 'If it's out of that barrow…'

'Look, I told you, they dug that up years ago. I should know, I spent most of my school time watching. It was big then, but look at it now.'

Owen nodded. The corner of the field was a muddy mass of hillocks and ruined ditches. The humped earth in the centre was still shoulder-high, but scarred and pocked with cavities, sprouting dock and brambles.

Jack Hughes shouldered the metal detector. 'Now as for that ring of your mother's – you'll have to get her to come up here and show me the spot. This is a twelve-acre field and we can't go over it all. I've got to give this machine back, you know.'

'I know.' Owen threw the rubbish into one of the ditches. Then, on second thoughts, he picked the bits out again and pushed them into his pocket.

They walked around the humps and hollows of the ruined barrow and climbed the gate. His uncle turned towards the farm. 'Tell her Sunday would be best. I'll have a bit more time then.'

'Right.'

'And if we're arrested, you can come and break us out of jail.'

Owen grinned, and turned away down the lane.

The wind met him at the corner, leaping into his face like an exuberant dog. Down below, the valley curved into its great wooded horseshoe, the slow river glinting through it, the houses strung out along the road to Llandogo. There too, in its green field on the riverbank, stood the roofless abbey, its arches rising like stone fingers placed delicately together at the tips. It always seemed unfinished, he thought, not ruined; it was so neat, with its mown grass, and the pillars and buttresses springing into the vast windy spaces of the nave, open to the sky and its scudding clouds. Through the east window he could see the dark woods on the crag, and a faint crescent moon hanging over them.

The lamps were lit in Tintern, the last tourist coach roaring out of the car park. He took the muddy little footpath along the river and then ran through the huddle of houses to one with a green door and a stunted rosemary bush outside it.

'At last!' his mother shouted from the kitchen as he slammed the door. 'Your tea's nearly frazzled. Hurry up.'

He sat at the table, pushing his sister's books aside. 'Where are they?'

'Chepstow. They went in for the shopping.' She came in and dropped a hot plate in front of him. 'Did Jack find my ring?'

'No.' He explained quickly, between mouthfuls.

'Ah, well,' his mother sighed, flitting past the door with a frying pan in her hand. 'It's all a lost hope, if you ask me. I'd love to find it, but it's like looking for a needle in a haystack.'

Owen knew she was still upset. 'It'll turn up,' he said firmly. 'We'll find it.'

52

When he had finished, he took his coat upstairs and tipped out the finds on the bed. None of them were any use. He picked up the disc and looked at it carefully. It was certainly metal of some sort, beaten thin, corroding and crumbling away at the edges. Might it be silver? He rubbed the surface gently with his sleeve. There were marks on it, very thin, incised lines; he could make out a circle, and a crescent, then some lines that whirled around each other. And at the edge, scratches, like strange stick-like letters. Nothing that made sense.

Downstairs, the door slammed. He wrapped the disc in his school scarf and put it in the drawer. Then he threw the rest of the stuff in the bin.

'Owen!' his sister screeched up the stairs. 'Come and see this! Quick!'

She sounded so excited that he went down deliberately slowly, one step at a time.

They were all in the kitchen; his father was holding something heavy, wrapped up in the plaid rug from the car. Owen hurried over.

'What is it?'

'A hare. The car must have hit it. Clear all those books off the table, Becky.'

Carefully his father laid the bundle down, put a hand inside and gripped tight. Then he pulled away the rug.

The hare crouched on the table, body rigid, ears flat. It was white, in full winter coat, its huge eyes round in the dim room, with the firelight flickering deep in them like tiny red stars. It was a large creature, its strong back legs braced against the table.

'White!' Owen said. 'That's odd.'

'It certainly is.' His father eased his grip gently. 'It might be an albino; you don't get mountain hares round here.'

The hare stared out at nothing. Its ears twitched.

'Doesn't seem to be hurt.' Mr Lewis felt over its skin carefully. 'Nothing broken. Just shock, I suppose. The way it loomed up in the road was terrifying – a white flicker in the moonlight, just on that bend by the quarry where the trees are thickest. I didn't feel a thump, but when we stopped the car and went back it was just sitting there, looking at us.'

'I think we went right over it,' Rebecca said. She reached out and touched the animal. It did not move as she slowly smoothed the stiff fur of its neck, and she smiled at the feel of it. 'Will it be all right?'

'Oh yes. We'll leave it in here tonight, in the warm. The cat can sleep in the shed for once. Now don't make a fuss of it, Beck.'

'I won't,' she said. But still her fingers stroked it, over and over.

All evening the hare lay in the box of straw by the fire. Rebecca gave it some water and a few lettuce leaves but it did not even sniff them. She and Owen played chess, and between moves she smoothed the hare and spoke to it, but it never turned its head. It sat still in the straw, watching the flickering firelight.

'Checkmate,' Owen said at last, happy, because he never usually won.

Rebecca turned. 'Well … no, it's not. I can go there.'

He tapped the bishop. 'Still in check. Your own fault. You can't concentrate because of that animal.'

He got up, yawning. 'Listen to the wind!'

The gale had been rising all evening; now it howled and hummed against the windows. A door upstairs was banging in the draught.

'There's nothing forecast.' Their father folded the newspaper and threw it down. 'Hopeless, these weather people. Now, time you went up into the hills.'

That was always his way of telling them to go to bed. Owen said goodnight and opened the door into the hall. A sudden gust of wind rattled against the windows.

'Coming from the west,' his father remarked.

Owen nodded. As he went out, he noticed the hare turn its head, for the first time. It looked at him. Its eyes were black.

✦✦✦

It was very late when Owen woke. The small gilt clock down in the hall was pinging quietly and he counted the strokes. Only three. But it had been some other noise that had woken him, not the clock, or even the wind that was roaring over the roof.

Something else.

He lay still. The room was dim, the window a paler square of darkness. He could see a star through a gap in the curtains, and the glow of next-door's porch light. Far off, a car droned up the valley.

He sat up, leaning one elbow on the pillow. There it was again – a low creak, coming from somewhere in the house.

The skin on the back of his neck prickled.

He swung his feet out into the cold air, pulled on trainers and a dressing gown and quietly opened the door. The landing was quiet, its furniture dark masses of shadow. His sister's door was open, just a slit, and he paused by it and breathed, 'Becky?'

No answer.

At the top of the stairs he waited, his hand tight on the smooth white ball of the bannister, his heart thumping softly.

The house stirred around him, its familiar creaks and ticks and sighs unheard. Nor the wind under the doors. It was the other sound he was waiting for, that long, oddly familiar creak of movement.

Inch by inch, silent, he came down the stairs. The kitchen door was open; a strange, pale light flooded out onto the table and the vase of evergreens, silvering his face as he crept nearer, and his hand as it reached for the knob.

In the room, something was moving.

Holding his breath, he edged the door wider and put his eye to the crack.

The kitchen was bright with moonlight; the curtains had been dragged back and an enormous full moon made the room a web of black and silver. Long rectangles of moonlight lay across the table and the newspaper and his chess pieces frozen in their game. He could see only half the room; the fireplace with its ashes, the window, the dresser.

Then the sweat on his face turned to ice.

A white hand had come out of the darkness and taken hold of the drawer handle; a long, thin hand with delicate fingers. Slowly, it drew the drawer open and began to dip and rustle inside, picking up forks and curtain rings and a watch and dropping them back with a click. As it pulled out a small mirror of his mother's, there was a pause; he heard a sound like an indrawn breath. Then the mirror was flung back. He could only see the hand, and the edge of a pale sleeve trimmed with fur.

The wind flung itself against the house; a window banged. In a surge of panic, Owen slammed the door wide and snapped on the light. In the sudden dazzle, something twisted and blurred and scuttled on the floor. He stared down at it.

The hare was sitting upright, looking at the moon.

It seemed bigger; the fur around its neck was bristling and stiff. It turned its head and looked at him, and sudden fear churned inside him like the wind whirling round the house. For a second, the stare held him, then he jerked back, slammed the door tight, turned the key and hurtled up the stairs.

His mother's voice caught him on the landing. 'Owen? What's wrong?'

'Nothing.' He was shaking. He gripped the brass rail of his bed and it was ice in his hot palms. 'Nothing. I just went down for a drink.'

✳ ✳ ✳

In the morning, Mr Lewis carried the box outside and set it down under the hedge. The grass was rigid with frost, and crunched underfoot. Owen, still chewing his toast, waited on the path.

'I still think it's a bit soon,' Rebecca complained. 'I think we should keep it for a bit.'

Her father shrugged. 'Owen's right. It's not a pet.'

She made a face at Owen but he ignored her. He was watching his father lift the creature out onto the frosty grass. The hare flattened its ears. It flopped one pace forward, and sat down.

'Off you go,' Mr Lewis muttered.

But the hare sat still.

'It doesn't want to go,' Becky murmured.

Go, Owen thought fiercely. *Whatever you are, go. Run away. Leave us alone.*

Mr Lewis stepped back. 'Leave it now. It'll soon go when it wants to.'

Owen went in and sat at the window, pretending to read. He was tired; he had spent the rest of the night sitting up in bed, listening to every creak in the house, every gust of wind, imagining the hare flopping up the stairs in the dark, waking with a crick in his neck at half past nine, when the horses from the riding school clopped past. And he hadn't told anyone. He couldn't.

All morning, he watched the hare. It didn't go. He knew it wouldn't. It sat in the melting frost, nose to the sky, the wind ruffling its fur. Not an animal. Something else, something other. Something deadly. He began to hate the sight of it, but he could not read, or get up and go out. It held his eyes with a real, undefined fear. He hadn't dreamed that cold hand searching the drawer. He had looked in there this morning – it was a mess, but that was normal. Still, he had seen it. It had been looking for something. He remembered the web of moonlight, silver and black.

At last, Rebecca marched downstairs. 'Well, I'm not leaving that poor animal out there,' she announced. 'It must be stunned.'

She unlatched the door.

'Don't!' Owen leapt up, nearly tipping the chair over. 'Leave it alone!'

She stared at him in astonishment. 'Don't be stupid. What's the fuss about?'

'Don't let it back into the house, Beck.'

'Why not?'

She was watching him with a strange, hostile look. How could he tell her? She would only laugh at him.

He shrugged. 'It gives me the creeps. It's not normal.'

She stared. 'You're mad, Owen.'

She went out and carried the hare in. 'The poor thing's dazed, that's all. It needs more time to recover. One more night should do it.'

One more night, Owen thought grimly. He watched her fingers smoothing the white fur; her face reflected in the hare's huge, upturned eyes.

＊＊＊

Later, in the cloisters of the abbey, the sun was warm on the stones. Owen leaned his head back and watched the tourists taking photographs in the nave, scattered in groups on the carpet of green grass. Year in, year out, the abbey stood there and the people came. Didn't they have ruined churches anywhere else, he wondered. Or poets that wrote about them?

He glanced up at the crag of the Devil's Pulpit

on the English side of the river. It was the stories that brought them, of course. The tales of monks and witches and real people who had lived long ago, and the trees, armies of them, guarding the border. Up there, the devil had screamed at the monks, thrown rocks, they said. All nonsense, of course. The trees up there were bending now, in the gale. A thin moon, faint as a smudge of chalk, hung over them.

The sight of it sat him bolt upright in shock.

The moon!

Last night it had been full!

He remembered it clearly, the huge circle of silver, the dark smudges of its seas and mountains.

What did it mean? How could the moon change or a hare be anything but a hare?

He shook his head and scrambled up, walking quickly through the arches into the booking office packed with shelves of mugs and tea towels and CADW guidebooks, out through the swing door, then breaking into a run along the river, as it swirled brown and swift under the hanging woods. Past the houses, across the road, dodging the cars, then up the lane to the farm, running hard now, dragging in breath as he raced uphill. The wind was with him. It pushed and buffeted him on, up the steep muddy lane between hawthorns and hollies.

The drone of the tractor met him at Cae Mawr; he leapt on the gate and waved, then swung over and raced across the furrows.

His uncle leaned out of the cab. 'You'll get covered in mud.'

'Never mind,' he gasped. 'Listen, that barrow...'

His uncle grinned. 'Still thinking about that?'

'But listen! Whose was it? What did they find in it?'

Jack Hughes cut the engine, climbed down and lit a cigarette. Smoke streamed in the wind. 'Well, not much. They were female remains, I remember that. Old, Bronze Age, maybe. There were a lot of little bits and pieces: ornaments, a buckle, brooches and the like. Most of it was badly corroded – just looked like little blue scraps to me, when they showed me. The best thing was a big cauldron, and there was a broken axle from a cart.'

'But you said it was called...'

'...Caer Ceridwen, yes. Ceridwen's Fort. Oh, you remember her, in one of those old folktales. She was a witch, a shape-shifter, maybe even a goddess. She turned herself into different creatures, hunting the lad who stole the magic from her cauldron.' He gazed out into the wind. 'Strange now, that this place should have had a woman's name all this time, and then to find a real woman in it. Where are you off to now?'

But Owen was already climbing the gate. 'Home!' he shouted. Then he turned. 'In that story. Did she catch the boy?'

'She caught him,' Jack Hughes yelled over the wind. 'There's no escaping her.'

***

The lanes were already darkening; the wind howling down the valley in all the moving branches of the trees. The lights of a cottage down a track flickered on as Owen raced by. Glancing back, he saw something pale glimmer in the lane behind him. For a second he saw it clearly: a white hare sitting upright in the shelter of the hedge. Then the wind gusted, flapping his coat collar and blowing dust into his eyes so that they watered and suddenly the road ran with flickering shapes: a slim dog, an otter, a flapping hawk, blurring one into the other, nearer and nearer under the roaring trees. Owen turned and fled into the darkness, racing along the lane, round the corner, breathless and aching to the giddy lip of the valley where he clung, winded, to a gatepost.

Below, the abbey was a black net pierced with arches; beside it, the river glinted with moonlight. Clouds moved on its rippling surface. Like a mirror, he thought, clutching his side. Like a mirror.

The village was dark as he stumbled down between the houses. The light from the kitchen dazzled him as he flung the door open and almost fell inside.

The box by the fire was empty.

'Where's the hare?' he gasped.

His father glanced over the newspaper. 'It's there, isn't it?'

Fear clutching him, Owen ran into the hall.

The hare was waiting at the top of the stairs, its white fur glistening, its eyes dark holes. It flopped slowly past him down the steps.

He ran up into his mother's bedroom. Every drawer and cupboard was open; clothes and jewellery were strewn on the bed and the floor.

Hurriedly, he picked things up, shoved them back. The others mustn't know. Whatever happened, they mustn't. He knew now that it was his fault, that he would have to sort it out.

When it was done, he went down and ate his tea. The hare was in its box, staring into the flames.

He sat opposite it, grimly.

Outside the gale lashed at the walls. The windows thrummed like taut wire.

His father came in at nine. 'The Anchor's closed early,' he said. 'River's rising fast – it must be raining higher up. And the wind in the abbey sounds like a choir of voices. I'd better put the shutters up on the back windows.'

All evening, Owen watched the hare and the hare watched him.

His mother laughed at the television. Rebecca lay curled in a chair with a book. Every now and then she reached down and stroked the white fur; once the hare moved, uneasily, and the wind screamed in the chimney.

All evening, Owen was never alone with it. Even when he tried to be the last one up, he was so tired that his mother made him go to bed. He splashed some water on his face, went into the bathroom, sat on his bed and waited.

The shapes of animals, flowing one into another, moved under his eyelids.

At half past two, a sound jerked him awake. Furious with himself, he opened the door quickly and peered out. The house was humming in the wind; the door to his sister's room was wide and moonlight was pouring through it. Clutching something in his hand, he went in.

Rebecca lay asleep, the pale light streaming over her. Next to the bed, looking down, stood a woman: tall, her hair woven into elaborate braids. She wore a straight, white dress pinned with a silver brooch at each shoulder. Her hand was stretched out; she had picked up a lock of Becky's brown hair from the pillow and was fingering it.

She looked up, her eyes dark and venomous. Behind her he glimpsed the open wardrobe, the crumpled clothes flung on the floor.

'Leave her alone,' he muttered.

The woman's eyes were black in the moonlight. 'Give me my mirror,' she said.

'Leave her alone. Leave us all alone and I'll give it to you.'

He brought his hand out from behind his back and held it out to her, the thin silver disc with its moon-marks and lost unreadable words. She moved quickly, but he drew back.

'Promise first. That you'll never come again.'

'It was you who came.' She stepped towards him. Her face was narrow, her lips pale in the unearthly light. 'You came and took what was mine. I am the pursuer. I have hunted you down and found you.'

She took the mirror out of his hand, and it glittered as she lifted it and looked in. Owen saw her face, to his astonishment, perfectly mirrored, as if the corroded metal was polished smooth. She turned it, and he saw himself, small and white-faced, and behind him the moon, huge in the window, and out there was the valley dark with trees, the abbey gone, the houses gone; only the trees, crowding to the river's edge, their dark undergrowth riddled with the paths of wolf and boar.

'We are all in here,' she said. 'Beast, man, spirit. Water and tree. Those who come and those who go. All reflected, as if in a tale, or a story.'

The metal slowly clouded.

Then there was only the hare, sitting white and still on the bedroom carpet.

After a moment, Owen turned and went downstairs, then through the kitchen to the back door. As he opened it, the cold wind struck him.

The hare flopped past him and sat on the doorstep, its great eyes staring out into the banging, flapping darkness.

'I'm sorry,' Owen said abruptly, 'about the barrow. I'll try and get them not to go there again.'

The hare looked at him. Then it bolted into the dark.

Before he closed the door, Owen put his head out and looked down at the abbey. A thin half moon balanced on its black shoulder. As he turned, he felt something cold as ice under his foot; it lay on the doorstep gleaming, and he bent and picked it up.

It was his mother's ring.

THE CHANGING ROOM

THE CHANGING ROOM

4

 First the tiny little kid threw me over her right shoulder.

I got up.

Then she threw me over her left shoulder.

I got up again. I went for my best move but she saw it coming, flipped my ankle, twisted my wrist and had me on my back before I could even breathe.

By now, even my bruises had bruises.

I scrambled up, breathless, and we bowed grimly to each other across the mat.

I had a sore back, a broken fingernail and a pain in my left ankle. The kid looked about six.

'Mmm.' The Judo coach put down his clipboard and folded his arms sadly. 'Well, I'm sorry, Chloe. I'm afraid you need a lot more practice before I can award a green belt. I think your coach has put you in for this a bit too early, to tell the truth.'

I nodded. He was right, and I'd thought that all along. But I was really fed up. It would have been great to go home with the belt, and now the twins would just make fun, and Dad would be disappointed, even though he wouldn't say so when I got back to the car.

I gathered up my stuff, said thanks, even to the annoying little kid, and went out into the corridor.

It was then I realised how late it was. The clock said 9.15. I'd been the last for the grading and everyone else in the building seemed to have gone home. The swimming pool was closed, and the dim corridor that led down to the changing rooms was empty.

I hurried down it, under the flickering lights.

The leisure centre had a sort of dusty, abandoned feel about it. I'd never been here before; it was out of the town, down a lane that had taken us ages to find, on the edge of a forest. We'd been so late I had changed into my kit in the car on the way. Now, when I reached the Ladies, I tried the handle and found it was locked.

Typical!

As I turned away, I saw there was a sign on

74

another door, a small dingy grey door in the corner. It said:

PRIVATE CHANGING ROOM
Strictly Members Only

I looked round but there was nowhere else and no one around so I opened the door and went in. Now I don't know about you, but I don't like changing rooms at the best of times. They smell, usually of old socks. People leave clothes around. There's always a dripping tap. And you never know who'll be in there.

This one was empty, and no posher than any other. In fact it was worse.

I shivered, because it was so damp and yes, it stank really bad. The tiles were greeny-grey and the ceiling was grey-green. The tap dripped, slowly, onto a brown stain in the sink.

I sat on the wooden bench and quickly started to take off my kit.

I would have liked a shower, but one look at the grimy floor made me shudder. I'd just have to stay sweaty. I hurried. The one light in the ceiling kept flickering as if it would go out any minute and leave me in the dark, which was not a nice thought, and I could hear an odd noise too, a sort of distant *clang* from far off in the building that sounded ominous and made me nervous.

What if I got locked in?

I didn't like that idea.

So I was glad when the other girl came in.

She was tall with short dark hair. She was dressed in white shorts and top and had a badminton racquet under one arm and a smart sports bag.

She looked at me. I sort of nodded back and hurried to pull on my jeans. She put her bag on the seat beside her. Then she said, 'You're new here.'

'Yes.'

'Haven't seen you before.'

'No, I just came for tonight.'

'Judo?'

'Yes. A grading. For a green belt.'

'Did you get it?'

'No.' I felt a bit annoyed saying that. In fact, I felt a bit annoyed having to talk at all, as most people don't talk in changing rooms, it's sort of an unspoken rule. But if she knew it, she ignored it.

And strangely, she just sat there, with no sign of getting changed.

I rummaged for my clean T-shirt.

'So you're not a member?' she said.

'No.'

That seemed to annoy her. 'Then you shouldn't be in here.'

'Oh. Well, the other room was locked and…'

'No, you don't understand.' She stood up. She was taller than I'd thought and suddenly she was very angry. 'You shouldn't have entered this room. It's against the rules.'

I stared. I felt uneasy. 'Like I said, sorry. I won't be long, I'm nearly ready.' I pulled my sock on. It was inside out but I didn't care; I was in a hurry now, because this weirdo was scaring me.

When I looked up, she was standing in front of the door.

'You have to make up for it,' she said.

I was dressed. I stood, leaving my bag on the bench and keeping my hands free. I may not have got the green belt, but I knew how to defend myself and no skinny girl was going to bully me. 'I'm going,' I said. 'Right now. Get out of the way.'

I turned to get my bag and dizziness came over me in a wave so intense my knees crumpled and I sat down with a thump.

The girl didn't move.

But her white kit was a dress now – had it been that before? And she wore a silver necklace at her throat and her nails were silver too.

'It's not that easy,' she said crossly. 'You have to do me a favour, and I know what it will be. We have to change.'

'Change?' I muttered.

She nodded. She came and sat opposite to me. 'This is the Changing room. You and I will change places. No one will know the difference.'

'Now wait a minute…' I said, but she didn't take a bit of notice.

'Actually, it works out really well for tomorrow. You are just what I need.'

'How can I change places with you? Are you mad?' I picked up my bag. I wanted to walk to the door but my legs wouldn't work. I felt as if I had been turned into something soft. As if I had been melted and poured out onto the bench.

The girl's smile was pure and cold as ice. She

looked as if she'd had the greatest idea of her life.

'Listen. This is what you have to do. I am the queen of a secret country. Every year I have to defend it against … a creature.'

'Creature?' I whispered.

'My enemy. My shadow. Her name is Hafgan. I can never defeat her because she's just as powerful as me and every year we fight like summer and winter and neither of us can defeat the other because we're equal. But now there's you. You will take my place. You will fight her and you will win.'

I laughed. 'I can't even get a green belt.'

'You're human. That will be enough.'

I went cold. 'Then … what are you?' I whispered.

She fixed me with her steely grey eyes. 'Someone you don't want to annoy any more than you already have. One thing – and this is so important. When you fight with her you must give her one fall and one only. No more! However much she taunts you. If you do any more, she will destroy you. Do you understand?'

'Yes, but…'

'Are you ready?'

'Look...'

'Or I could punish you for entering this room.'

She was crazy. A maniac. I just had to agree and get out of here. 'All right,' I said soothingly. 'All right. Let's change. Let's do it. Anything you say.'

I blinked.

What...?

How...?

I was looking at myself.

I watched myself stand and pick up my bag and go to the door, but when my body spoke, it had my voice but her words.

'Come on, then,' she snapped.

And when I looked down, I gave a shriek of astonishment and terror, because I was tall and my nails were silver and I was wearing a white dress. My hair was as dark as midnight. My skin itched like icicles, my heart was beating all wrong and my nerves tingled. I could see shapes and shadows in the corners of my eyes. The room was a forest of trees. The bench was a fallen log. The lockers glittered behind a splashing waterfall.

Even the tongue inside my mouth was strangely thin and serpentine. I felt as if starlight had flooded inside me and if I spoke it would turn into music. But when I did it was just her voice.

'*What have you done to me!*'

She smiled my smile. 'Don't worry. Just win the fight and everything will be fine.' She took my hairbrush out of my bag and shoved it in the back of a locker. 'That will be my excuse for coming back. Sunset tomorrow, be here, and we'll change back. But remember, just one fall. *Whatever happens*, whatever Hafgan says, don't do anything more.'

Then she was walking out and down the corridor. I gasped and stood and ran after her under the flickering lights that went out as I passed, but I couldn't seem to catch her up, and when I got out of the building it was dark and the moon was shining.

I stared. I saw Dad waiting by the car. She ran to him and he put his arm round her and asked something. She shook my head and he laughed

81

and rubbed her hair – my hair! – and then they both got in the car and drove away.

I stood there, devastated.

I had seen myself.

From the outside.

And now it was even more terrifying, because if my body had gone, what was left of me?

I looked round.

The leisure centre shrank and twisted and blurred. It became a dark castle of high turrets and walls overgrown with ivy and honeysuckle. A moat glinted round it and over the moat was a drawbridge.

I was beyond surprise. I walked over the bridge and stared to explore.

I had never been in such a place. Room after room, chamber beyond chamber. Some gloriously splendid with silken hangings and golden furniture, and others that were dark and cobwebbed and bare as the poorest cottage in a fairytale. I walked down corridors that ran for miles and through galleries hung with painted faces that moved and whispered.

In one high turret, I looked through the window

and saw the sea, wide and black, its waves crashing on rocks below the castle walls. And in another I looked out on an ice field, blue with shadows, stretching in glacial silence to the horizon. I stared, fascinated. How was that possible?

In other rooms there were meals laid on long tables, and fires lit in the chimneys. White doves fluttered in vast cages. A black cat slept on a silver bed.

Finally I came to a small sitting room and collapsed into a blue satin chair by one of the fires and stared at the flames which burned without cracking or spitting. Something told me that eating even a mouthful of the food would be a mistake, but I wasn't even hungry. All I could think of was her, at my house. Was she lying on my bed now, dressed in my pyjamas? Looking at my books? Drinking my mug of hot chocolate?

Being kissed goodnight by my mum and dad?

It made me feel so lonely and far away from everyone, as if I would never get back there.

I must have fallen asleep in that chair, but when I woke up I was lying in a huge bed with red curtains all around it, and that scared me. I scrambled up and slid off it, and there was daylight coming in through a wide-open glass door.

Dawn!

At once I ran. It took ages to find a way out, but then I hurried through the door and down some steps onto a wide green lawn, and far across it I could see a small river glinting brightly.

As I raced towards it, I saw someone else approaching on the other side. At first it was just a shiver in the low morning mist, then I could see a blurred figure. The mist stretched it to a huge height, so that I was terrified, then dissolved it to a frail shadow, winged and sinister. As it came to the river, I saw it was an exact copy of the girl I had met. Of me. Or rather, my opposite.

She had white blonde hair, and she wore a black dress. Her nails were black and her necklace glittered like jet. But her face was identical and her voice, when she spoke, was like an echo.

'So you've come.'

'Yes,' I said.

She stepped into the river.

I did the same.

It was so strange. We waded out until the water

was around our waists, and yet it didn't feel cold or wet. We faced each other. Her eyes were sharp with anger.

'Every year,' she said, 'the same.'

I nodded. I had no idea what to do, but suddenly she grabbed me, she had hold of my arms and she was trying to force me under the water. She was incredibly strong! For a moment I slid and almost lost my balance; I gasped and toppled and she grinned and pulled harder and the water was up to my chin and I swallowed some of it and it tasted like silver.

Then I moved. I did the hold I had practised for the grading, took a grip on her and put my hip in and lifted her and flipped her and she was down.

She went into the water with a screech of fury.

I stepped back, grinning.

When she scrambled up, the water was pouring out of her hair but even so she wasn't wet.

I turned and walked out of the river.

She stared. 'Where are you going?'

'Home.'

She shook her head. 'What…? This is wrong. You're not her. You're a stranger. A human!'

'Yes,' I said, facing her, but backing away.

'Come back! You can't just leave! We haven't finished! Nothing is decided.'

'Yes, it is,' I said. 'I've won. I did what I had to do. Now I'm going home.'

'Wait! Listen! Don't you see this is wrong? It will break the balance! It will twist the world askew! Winter and summer, cold and heat, they have to balance. When humans interfere, everything goes wrong. Come back and let me throw you down too, and it will be as it should be.'

I turned my back and I walked away. It was strange, because actually I wanted to go back. What she said made sense, and I felt guilty and unsure. Also, I wanted to throw her again, and again, like that annoying little kid had done to me in the grading. I wanted to be a real winner, and I knew I could have done it.

Then her argument changed. 'I can make you anything,' she hissed. 'I can give you power. You will never lose to anyone in your world again.'

I nodded, still walking. Was I doing the right thing? How did I know which of them was telling the truth?

86

But it was too late now, because with every step her voice became shriller and stranger and thinner, and then between one step and another it was just the whining of gnats over the river. When I stopped and looked back she was a shimmer of darkness on the water, that dissolved to mist and was gone.

I felt really bad.

As if I'd killed something, or broken something fragile.

And yet it wasn't my fault. All I wanted was to get home.

I looked up, and there in front of me was the leisure centre, standing in the car park against the trees, and it was dark here, with the lamps lit, as if a whole day had gone by.

I ran into the building, along the corridors and crashed through the door of the Members' Changing Room.

She – I – was sitting on the bench. She was wearing my favourite top, the black one one I keep for best. 'Who said you could put that on?' I said, furious.

She ignored me. 'Have you done what I asked?'

I shrugged. 'I threw her down once. If that's a win, then I won. But it doesn't seem fair.'

She laughed. 'Only humans care about fair.'

I frowned. 'That's not what she said.'

'She's my opposite. We never agree.'

She stood up.

And then…

I blinked.

What?

How…?

I was wearing the black top, and these were my hands and this was my face, and the tongue in my mouth was the right shape, and the room looked just like an ordinary room.

But the music and the light were gone from inside me, and for a moment I looked for them, and was sorry I couldn't find them.

The girl grinned. She threw the hairbrush at me and opened the door. 'Don't come here again,' she said.

'Don't worry!' I growled. 'I won't!'

✳✳✳

Outside, Dad was playing one of his CDs in the car.

'Got it?' he muttered.

I nodded, and tossed the hairbrush on the back seat. All of a sudden I felt very tired and really hungry. 'Can we stop somewhere on the way back? I'm starving.'

'Well, I'm not surprised. You only picked at your food.'

As the car purred out of the car park, I said quietly, 'Apart from that, was I … the same as usual this morning? Last night?'

He shrugged. 'Just the same. Why?'

'No reason.' I looked out of the window, frowning. Maybe I had dreamed the whole thing? How could it have been possible, anyway?

'Except, of course, for what you did to your room,' he said.

'My room?'

'Yes. I mean, that was so extraordinary! Where did you get those colours! Those drawings all over the walls! I don't know how you could sleep in that. Your mother screamed when she saw it. It's like something out of a horror story.'

89

I stared at him, a little scared. 'Great. Well, I'll just have to paint over it, I suppose.'

I stared out at the dark woods beside the road. What had she done to my room? What castles and creatures awaited me on the walls? Suddenly I really wanted to find out. Maybe even to go back to that strange place, if I could find a way...

I was quiet a long time. Then I said, 'Dad?'

'Mmm?'

'That leisure centre.'

'What about it?'

'How do you get to be a member?'

SGILTI LIGHTFOOT

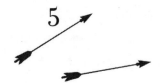

5

'Knife has gone into meat, drink into horn, and a thronging in Arthur's court.'

'Yes, yes, I'm sure it has,' I snapped, 'but they sent for me.'

The gatekeeper stopped picking his teeth with the point of his knife and stared. 'You? What would they want with an underfed little runt like you?'

I pushed past him. 'At least I'm not too drunk to find out.'

He aimed a kick, but I was already in the pavilion.

You could certainly call it a thronging. Bards and harpers sang in the dim smoke; there was a magician spinning blue and green rings of light, a dog fight, the hot stink of meat and spices, the clamour of noise and laughter and boasting – even a wrestling match in one uproarious corner.

They were all there, all the war band. Cai and

Bedwyr; Osla Big Knife, slightly drunk and waving his cup; Cynddylig the guide and Menw the spell-master; Gwalchmai with his scarlet cloak; Morgan, tall and slender, the pet snake writhing up her arm.

Arthur sat among them, his hands rubbing the carved heads on the arms of his chair, his gaze fixed and remote. Someone was talking to him, but I don't think he was listening. In all that din, I doubt he could have heard.

Then he saw me and his eyes became alert, quite suddenly.

I pushed my way up to him. 'Lord?'

He gave me his hard, sombre stare. 'You're the lad Sgilti?' He twisted his head and yelled, 'Is this the boy?'

Talk subsided. The magician dropped his rings; they fell into the straw and spluttered out with a scorching hiss. Everyone looked at me.

'Yes.' Cai came and leaned on the back of the chair. 'That's him.'

For a moment, I thought I had done something wrong. Then Arthur nodded. 'He's small, lithe, but looks strong enough. He might do.'

Cai turned, lazily. 'Give him a drink.'

Nervously, I sipped the warm, spiced wine someone pushed into my hand. Outside, the sounds of the camp drifted through the noise: horses at their ropes, the eternal crackle of fires. I noticed a thin man with gangly arms sitting on a stool at Arthur's feet. He was the only one not looking at me.

'Now,' Arthur said grimly, 'how long have we been besieging this fortress?'

I shrugged. 'Days and nights are the same now, Lord. About nine months?'

'A year.' He curled his fist. 'A whole year of darkness. And the fortress not even scratched.'

I nodded, remembering the day the darkness had come, spreading and spilling over the hills and forests, like ink soaking a map. I had been outside my father's forge at home when I had glanced up to see what covered the sun. When I looked down, I hadn't even been able to see my own skinny feet.

Since then, there had been no light. No sun, no moon, no stars, nothing to tell night from day. We lived among black fields, in rooms acrid with constant smoke. Crops curled in the furrow; cattle pined and died; birdsong was almost forgotten.

So Arthur had gathered his war-band, and we had marched for ten days into the heart of the blackness and found this place – the fortress, its black stones swallowing even the gleam of torches we held up to it. No one knew how high it was. The walls reared up, silent and empty; smooth fire-scarred blocks that grapples would not cling to, the moan of the wind sounding round them.

'There's talk,' I said doubtfully, 'in the camp. About a sorcerer.'

It was Cai who answered, with his sharp grin. 'We know plenty of those. Yes, we know who made the darkness. His name is Llwyd ap Cil Coed. He did something of the kind once before.' He gave a quick glance at Arthur. 'This is his revenge on us.'

Arthur said, 'I hear you're a good tumbler. Show us.'

I stared, astonished. 'Here?'

'Now.'

The heat of the wine scorched my cheeks. I looked round; they were all watching.

'Come on,' Bedwyr snapped. 'Let's see.'

I stood up and pulled off my jerkin. Was this all they wanted, then, some after-meat entertainment from the scrawniest boy in the war band? Surely they had enough harpers and dancers without picking on me?

The floor was clear. I stood lightly on my hands and ran a few steps, my hair falling in my eyes. Then I stood and flipped forward, once, twice and then backwards as high and light as I could.

'Stand on one hand,' Morgan said, coming forward from the shadows.

I obeyed, lifting my left hand carefully from the ground, feeling the ache in my right, the growing wobble in my body. Quickly, I rolled and jumped up.

'And is it true,' Gwalchmai asked quietly, 'that you climbed the siege ladder yesterday and jumped as it fell?'

I nodded, warily.

'You don't fear heights?'

'No, Lord.'

He raised one eyebrow at Arthur.

'Oh yes,' the emperor said. 'Yes, he'll do. Agreed?' He glanced around; the war band eyed each other and nodded, the edges of their faces red in the flame-light.

Arthur looked down. 'And you? Do you agree?'

The thin man on the stool stirred. His long arms were wrapped around his knees, his fingers locked together. He shrugged. 'If he has the nerve. Which I doubt.'

I glared at him angrily. 'Whatever it is, I'm not afraid to try.'

Arthur laughed and leaned back. 'Explain it to him.'

Cai nodded. 'Look, Sgilti, all methods of attack on the fortress have failed. Whatever sorcery guards it repels ladders and siege towers; its walls are battered with rams and missiles and magic and are not even cracked. They can't be burned, and however deep we dig we can't find their foundations. And, until now, we thought it was too smooth to climb.'

He pointed down. 'This man is called the Spider. Perhaps you can guess why.'

I did. I had begun to understand.

Morgan came and stood in front of me, one long braid of hair swinging over her shoulder. She took my hand; her fingers were long and white. 'We've used fire-arrows to see high. There's one window that might do. It is high – very high. We think it might be wide enough – just – for a thin man to climb through. Or a boy.'

'That's why you want me?'

She smiled. 'Arthur has many heroes. They are all too big.'

'We need two,' Arthur said, 'in case one falls. Someone must open the gate for us.'

I nodded, watching the Spider unfurl himself and stand up: a thin, spindly man, his brown hair cropped short. 'I still say he won't make it,' he muttered.

Arthur looked at me. 'He must.'

✳✳✳

Later, when we stood alone at the wall, I watched the man check the rope: the finest and strongest the company could find.

'Why didn't you want me?'

He looked up. 'I didn't want anyone. If you don't get up there, I'll have to manage without you anyway.'

I held my anger tight inside me: a small hard knot.

The air was very cold, with little noise from the camp. Everyone was gone to the gates. The dim wall of the fortress leaned out above me. I imagined its invisible battlements, embrasures and stairs, its remote pinnacles and airy bridges spanning the gaps from tower to tower.

The Spider flexed his long arms. 'Now, then.'

'Good luck.'

'I don't need luck. Keep it for yourself.'

He gave a quick spring and clung to the wall, hands and feet splayed, then began to climb with astonishing speed, feeling with fingers and elbows, toes and knees for invisible crannies. In the silence, faint scuffles came down to me. For a second, he even looked like a spider, a spindly-jointed shape clinging and jerking its way up into the dark.

I crouched in the lee of the wall, the wind flapping my black coat. Soon I'd have to follow – but at least I'd have the rope.

After a while, I heard a faint tap, and something thudded near my feet. I groped for it and found a small peg. That was useless. Nothing would pierce the fortress, Cai had said. The Spider must have found that out for himself; the tapping stopped and there was silence.

'All right?' I whispered.

No answer. He was probably too high to hear.

I must have been half asleep when the rope hit me silently on the shoulder; a thin line snaking down the wall. I gave it a swift tug and felt the answering twitch. He had done it!

Quickly, I looped the line round my waist, tied it tight and swung my legs up onto the wall.

The rope held me, a ring of comfort. Hand over hand, I began to haul myself up.

It didn't take long for my arms to start getting tired. The ache grew worse, the muscles forming hard knots of pain. I stopped, swaying, gasping for cold air, but the weight seemed heavier like this. It was better to keep going, so I heaved myself up, each hand-grip a terrible wrench and tug, the slither of the rope scorching through my gloves. At last, through a wave of fatigue, I felt my foot settle on something soft, like a cushion of moss on the wall. I put my weight on it; it yielded, and then held.

With a moan of relief, I pulled myself upright

against the wall. There were more of the things, well-spaced for my hands and feet. For a long time I clung there, splayed against the black surface, my cheek pressed to the black stones. I could smell tiny lichens clinging in the crannies. Up here the wind ruffled my hair; small campfires flickered below.

After a while I felt better and began to wonder what I was standing on. What had managed to break the sorcery of the fortress? I slid my hand along, feeling carefully. It was something sticky; a whole mass of threads, thin and tough. I followed them, touching gently; they spread from stone to stone, stretched like skeins of fine silk.

A web.

How had he made it?

I shivered, and at the same time the rope went taut and then tugged gently. I wound the slack around me. At least if I fell I'd finish here. Better to dangle like a broken puppet than hit the ground. Then I took hold, and swung out.

The ache came back at once. Above, I could see the wall jutting out steeply; I hauled myself underneath, hoping the rope had not frayed against the edge. I had to take my feet from the wall and spin giddily in the dark for a few seconds, before I could swarm up onto the overhang.

There was a sloping roof, broad enough to stand on, carved with strange grinning heads. From here, I could see the wall ascend again into blackness, and the ghostly line of the rope, as it passed an arrow slit just visible above.

I began to doubt then that I could do it. Every muscle already ached; my hands were sore, my legs weak. The thought of that long fall into blackness wouldn't keep away. But I couldn't stay here. And Arthur was depending on me.

By the time I reached the arrow slit, I was exhausted. My arms were leaden, wind whipped out my hair. Wedging my feet in the thin slit, I hung there, careless of danger, my mind sick and spinning.

'Hurry up!' the voice hissed down the wall. Glancing up, I saw the window just above, and his dark shape leaning out. Then I made a mistake.

I looked down.

I've never been afraid of heights – I told the war band the truth. But that utter emptiness, the flickers of fire so far below – it made tiny cold terrors unfurl in my stomach.

Then a light was shining in my face!

With a jerk of alarm, I leapt from the sill and crashed into the wall, cursing my stupidity. Inside the building, a candle flame was moving, coming closer, the bright glow in the black arrow slit.

The rope twisted and thrummed, trapping my fingers; I dragged them free and grabbed again, biting my lip from the pain. Then I clung tight, swaying.

The candle came to the window. I could see the hand that held it, a thin hand with long nails. It stayed, as if the figure was waiting, listening. Was this the Sorcerer, in his fortress?

I hung on grimly, my hands scorching, a raw pain in my stomach.

I couldn't move.

I was finished.

Then the rope jerked, and wonderfully, I felt it rise and lift me up. I was dragged up the wall in a silent series of jerks and sharp drops that sent fear gasping through me. The arrow slit fell away below. I came up through darkness, a swinging nausea of rope and stone, to a hand that grabbed me and hauled me over the sill to a solid floor, where I collapsed, a shivering heap.

'Didn't think you'd do it,' a voice whispered in my ear. 'You can let go of the rope now.'

But I had to force my fingers to open; the joints seemed set. My gloves were torn to ribbons, the skin of my palms red and sore.

'Drink this.'

The Spider's fingers offered a small flask out of the dark. The liquid in it was hot and sweet; it made me cough.

'Now get up!' He hauled me to my feet. 'Walk about. Hurry.'

Slowly, the trembling in my legs steadied; I could stand, and then walk. Beside me there was a sudden spurt of flame; he lit the torch and it crackled and spat, throwing red light leaping over our faces.

He looked at me. 'I suppose I should say I was wrong.'

'You can say what you like,' I muttered, rubbing my wrenched arms. 'You could start with how you put those cobwebs on the walls.'

I hadn't meant it to blurt out like that, but in the flame-light I saw his thin smile. 'My secret.'

'And there's someone in here. Just below.' I told him about the hand that had held the candle. He shrugged and stood up. 'We must leave that to Arthur. Our task is to find the gates.'

The torch showed we were in a small hall with thick pillars that lost themselves in the gloom overhead. There was a door in the wall, and I tried the handle, cautiously. It opened.

We looked out into a black, silent corridor. Cold airs drifted against my face.

I walked in the Spider's long shadow, thinking of all the rooms and chambers about us, of the hand with the candle. But there was no sound, nothing leapt out at us. We felt our way down twisting stairs, through halls littered with the dark shapes of furniture, one chamber totally webbed with curtains of silk, all frayed and worn to holes so that when I put my hand on one, it crumpled, with a faint puff of sound.

As we went down, the air grew blacker. The light of the torch became pale and sickly, finally useless. The Spider threw it down in disgust and it went out.

Blackness closed in.

Now we had to feel. Progress became a slow weary shuffling, inch by inch, along an invisible wall that led up right, and left, and down endless steps.

Finally the Spider stopped, and I bumped into him.

'It's impossible,' he snarled. 'We could be any-where! Walking in circles, no doubt.' His voice hung, as if there were a high roof. We realised all at once that we were in a very large room, a hall, bitterly cold. In this place, the darkness was more than lack of light; it was a breathing thing, alive, pressing against us. This was the heart of the fortress.

Suddenly, I took my fingers off the wall and stepped away. At once I lost all bearing, was surrounded by nothing.

'Keep still,' the Spider snapped. 'If we lose each other…'

'We won't. You can make sure of that.'

I heard him laugh. 'Maybe. But where are you going? We need to find the gates, to go down. We should move along the wall and find the next set of steps. It won't be out there in the middle.'

'Something's out there,' I whispered, staring into the gloom. 'I know it is. I can feel it. Let me go and look. You can always pull me back.'

'No rope.'

'You don't need a rope.'

There it was again, his rustle of amusement. 'No wonder Cai picked you,' he said. 'All right. Come a bit closer.'

I moved, banging awkwardly against him. His hand groped for mine. In the inky stillness, he took off my glove and I felt a cold touch in the centre of my palm. A thin thread lay across my skin, slightly sticky as I touched it.

Without a word, I turned and stepped out into the dark. The invisible line stretched behind me.

I had stepped into nowhere. Darkness was all about me, a weight against my hands and face; I had to wade through it, push against it. Each step was an effort. My feet slid over the smooth floor, feeling for pits and holes, deep wells that might be only inches away.

And then I bumped into something.

Heart thudding, I stopped. Faint echoes faded round the hall.

'What is it?' the Spider hissed, from far away.

'I don't know.'

Carefully, reluctantly, I put out my hand.

I touched a cold, smooth surface. My fingers travelled across it. When I felt the other thing, I jerked back, with a shiver of surprise.

After a long second, I touched it again. It was an edge, a curved edge, not metal… Glass? Gently, I fingered it. As my thumb moved up, it dislodged something light and smooth that fell back into place with a click. With both hands, I felt for it.

It was a small globe, on some kind of stand. I lifted it off and held it between my palms. It was very light. My fingers arched around it. Whatever it was made of was bitterly cold; my skin stuck to it.

This was the heart of it, this small ball. I held it, while the darkness breathed around me. Then, deliberately, I let it fall.

As it smashed, light exploded: a scatter of glass. I stood in a sudden blinding dazzle of colour, my eyes watering with the pain, staring at a great hall, flagged with stone, hung with festoons of glorious scarlet cloth, full of the echoes of some great cry ringing from roof to floor. Before me stood a white marble table, scattered with black shiny pieces of broken glass. Behind, one hand still on the wall, his face smudged with dirt and utter astonishment, stood the Spider, and between us through the air drifted a frail silver line, glittering in the sunlight from the windows.

In all the rooms and corridors of the fortress, the echoes faded into silence.

For a second we looked at each other, too over-awed to speak. Then I wiped a dirty hand over my face and grinned at him. It would be very easy now to find the gates.

 The mirror was nearly as tall as he was.

It was oval, the frame incredibly ornate, wreathed with leaves, small cherubs, scrolls and flowers.

Daniel reached out and touched the glass thoughtfully; it had a slightly smoky look. He scratched it with a fingernail. Not dirt. Something in the silvering, or its age most likely. Like everything in the house, it was old.

He looked at himself, and frowned. The bruise was yellow, with purple edges. It looked swollen and, if he touched it, it hurt. Carefully, he jutted his jaw out sideways a few times, and each time the familiar ache came and went.

His mother came out of the dining room, dragging the vacuum cleaner. 'Admiring yourself?'

He shrugged in the mirror. 'Not much to admire.'

'Too right. It must have been some game.'

'I suppose so.'

She paused a moment, looking, then she pushed the vacuum cleaner into the room Mrs Paulson still called the parlour. After a second, the machine erupted into its hoarse roar.

He touched the bruise. It wasn't from rugby. Perhaps she guessed that. It was from Michael Fairfax.

Once they had been friends, had sat next to each other in class. Now things were different. Michael had changed. He was still unpredictable, annoyingly cool, good for a laugh. But these days his jokes were getting … well, a bit much. Like taking Mrs Lewis' keys. He'd lifted them out of her handbag on the desk, while he was behind her. Most of the class hadn't noticed, but Daniel had seen, and Michael had just winked at him. It had almost been a threat. Once Daniel would have been delighted and scared and maybe shocked, secretly, but now he just felt a distaste that surprised himself.

He looked at his narrow face. 'You're getting old,' he said.

Deep in the mirror, he noticed something small. It was a blur of shape, as if the smoky effect had gathered there. It was difficult to say what it looked like, as it seemed to change as he tried to focus on it. For a moment, he glanced behind him, but the dim hallway was empty. He turned back and brought his eyes up close to the glass.

The tiny shape shifted, unmistakably.

✳✳✳

In the morning, he woke early, feeling restless. His room seemed full of light and birdsong, even with the curtains closed; he tugged them aside and knelt up on the bed, looking out. The garden glittered with melting frost. Yellow drifts of daffodils shone under the trees, and a pale sun gleamed through the black branches. He got up quickly, pulling on his uniform, listening to the chirp of sparrows, the warbles and clicks of starlings in the chimney, the creamy lament of some distant robin.

Coming out of his room, the rest of the house was silent. His mother's door was closed; her alarm didn't go off until seven and it was just before that. Mrs Paulson slept in the master bedroom below, a huge room filled with a dark four-poster bed that his mother said was worth a fortune and was a devil to clean, with all those curtains.

He went downstairs humming, running his hand down the smooth wooden rail. Today he'd avoid Michael. Talking to him was useless. And if there was any trouble about those keys, he didn't want to be a part of it. He jumped down into the hallway and went along to the kitchen door. Then, puzzled, he came back.

The blur in the mirror had grown. He was sure of it, even in this dim light. Now it was about the size of his fist, and he could see what it was, ghostly next to his own face.

A bird.

It was poised, wings up, as if frozen in flight, and it was inside the glass. He looked behind the mirror. There was nothing, and besides, how could a bird just hang like that, in mid-air, without moving? He touched the smooth surface, puzzled; thought of negative images, holograms. But the mirror had to be Victorian, if not older.

He was still looking at it when his mother's alarm went off, a tiny whine high in the house.

The restlessness stayed all through school. In Chemistry, he let the mysteries of the periodic table drift over his head, staring out at the wood on the hill. The sky was almost too blue, and even from here he could hear birdsong and smell the spring air with its scent of freedom.

'Daniel?' Dr Ross put the homework down on the edge of the table.

He felt foolish. 'Sorry.'

'Not a bad piece of work. You can do better, though.'

It was a B. He looked through it. He and Michael had always done the Chemistry together; he'd needed the help. Everything came easily to Michael. Too easily.

Around him, the class were swapping marks; a few people asked what he'd got and he said, 'B' and clipped the papers into his file. Outside, a class was trooping across the courtyard, Michael's class, the one he should never be in. And there he was, on his own at the end, his hair gleaming in the sun. For a moment he looked like he used to. Then he glanced up and saw Daniel and grinned. Pointing his hand like a gun, he pulled an imaginary trigger.

On the bus, it was hard to avoid him. He had the gang with him, and Daniel stared grimly through the windows at fleeting hedges and fallow brown fields.

Girls giggled at the back. Then Michael's voice came from a seat behind. 'I've still got those keys, Dan.'

Daniel glared at the countryside, silent.

'What do you think I should do with them?'

'You know what I think.'

'Sorry?' The voice was mockingly polite. 'Didn't quite catch that.'

Furious, Daniel turned. Michael was sprawled in the seat and his face had that hard, deliberately vacant look that Daniel loathed. 'I said, you know what I think! You should give them back. Just leave them on her desk.'

Michael leaned back, still gazing at him. He put his feet up, crossed at the ankles. 'Don't you learn?'

Daniel knelt. 'Don't you?' he hissed fiercely.

'You're the one with the bruise.'

'Because yours don't show. Don't be a fool. What can you do with the stupid keys?'

Michael glanced around casually. 'I could use them.'

The bus went quiet. Tom James and the little, sly one, Hughes, came clambering over the seats.

'Use them how?' Tom muttered greedily.

'How else?' Michael kept his eyes on Daniel. 'Get into her house. Take a look around.'

Daniel went cold. 'She'll have changed the locks.'

'No. She's using the spare set. Thinks these are at home. I heard her tell Davies.' His voice was light, his smile enigmatic.

'You can't!' The bus lurched. Daniel grabbed the steel bar across the window. 'What's the point?'

Michael grinned. 'Yeah. Exactly.'

Daniel swallowed his shock. It would only make things worse to let him see it. Michael liked to shock. It opened him up like sun on a daisy. Instead, he tried to be cold. 'I never had you down for a thief.'

The gang giggled. Michael smiled. 'Perhaps you never knew me very well.'

'I thought I did. Once.' They stared at each other, an icy minute. Then Daniel turned away.

119

✸✸✸

The bird had grown. He looked at it as soon as he got in and, after he'd dumped his coat and bag, he came back and stared at it again.

It was closer. Closer than this morning.

The wings had moved too, spread flat now, taking up nearly the width of the mirror. From one angle it might just be a glimmer, a trick of the light, but face-on he could see it clearly: the bird's white feathers, its dark eye and open beak.

It was coming towards him.

He took a step back, into a patch of sun from the fanlight.

Not possible.

'Daniel?' The sudden call made his heart thump. He turned and went into the sitting room.

Mrs Paulson had moved her wheelchair to the window; she sat with her small hands lying on the tapestry frame, the needle stuck into one corner of her work. 'I thought it was you. Would you mind opening the window? Just a bit? I'd like to hear the birds.'

He came over and tugged it up, and a breeze

lifted the faded silk flowers on the table. 'You could do with some new ones,' he said, looking at them.

'Daffodils would be nice. From the garden.' She breathed in, satisfied. 'Smell that. That's spring, Daniel, take it from me!'

He nodded, looking down at her. Mrs Paulson was eighty, but she seemed younger. Her hair was still dark, though he didn't know if that was dye. She wore a blue dress and a cardigan pinned at the neck by an expensive cameo, and she sat upright. She couldn't walk, but she was a lightning chess player, and had taught him to play backgammon and a dozen other forgotten Victorian games. Now, he said, 'Mrs P. That mirror in the hall...'

'Mmmm?'

'How old is it?'

'How old?' She smiled, roguishly. 'It was a wedding present. That makes it fifty at least. Whatever do you want to know that for?'

He shrugged. 'Have you ... ever noticed anything odd about it?'

'Odd?'

'Sort of ... things in it. That aren't.'

121

Mrs Paulson turned and looked at him. Then she said, 'Wheel me out there, Daniel. This minute.'

He did, taking care to avoid the doorframe, and as they came to a halt in front of the mirror, his mother let herself in through the front door and joined them.

'Why are we all looking at ourselves?'

'We're looking at the mirror,' Daniel muttered, feeling foolish.

Mrs Paulson shook her head. 'I can't see anything odd.'

'Neither can I. Not now.'

His own face stared at him. He scowled at it, annoyed.

But by bedtime the bird was back. It was huge, filling the mirror, its head pressed sideways against the glass as if in panic, the small black eyes wide. Frozen, it hung there, and he could see nothing but the trapped bird, its downy feathers flat, each barb clear.

It was trying to get out.

He watched his own dark shadow reflected over it, and a shudder of fear ran down his back, so that he raced upstairs away from it, leaving it behind.

In his pyjamas, he sat on the bed, thinking. No one else had noticed it. That didn't mean it wasn't real. It was an image; something that had maybe happened long ago. The mirror had preserved it, like a slowed-down film.

For an hour he lay in bed staring at the wall, unable to sleep. He heard his mother come up quietly, and the door of her room shut. The light went out. Darkness closed in on him.

The old house creaked and shifted, and outside a light rain pattered on the windows. He lay still, tense, as if every nerve was strained, waiting for something, something he didn't know he was waiting for until he heard it.

Fluttering.

It was soft and crisp, far below. The horrible, soft scuttering of stiff feathers, of a beak and claws, scrabbling, tapping, the thump of its wings.

He stood it for about ten minutes.

When he sat up, he was sweating and cold, all at once. He pulled on his dressing gown and went out, quietly on to the attic landing in his bare feet. Up here the carpet was old, worn to holes. He crept down the narrow staircase to the wide landing of the first floor, where the furniture was dark and portraits of Mrs Paulson's family looked down at him disapprovingly.

At the bottom was the mirror. He could see it from up here in the shadows of the hall, one edge of its frame glinting in the lamplight from the street.

The hall was long and dark. Something bumped and fluttered down there.

He came down the stairs one at a time. On the last he paused, the brass stair rod icy against his heel, the carpet soft and warm and thick. Then he came round and faced the mirror.

The bird was moving.

It fluttered desperately against the glass, the scrabble of its tiny claws loud and hard. It was so close now that he couldn't see it all; the edges of its wings were beyond the sides of the frame. It beat and flapped in a wild, mindless panic.

He put his hands up, but the glass was smooth and hard. The frame fitted close; he tried to squeeze his fingernails in, then gripped the sides tight in frustration. The bird would kill itself. Perhaps it had killed itself.

He stepped back. 'Come on,' he whispered, his voice fierce and low. 'Come on! Come out! You can do it. *Come out!*'

The bird fluttered and beat towards him, became bigger. Its great chest filled the mirror; he saw every barb and feather huge and close as it struggled and fought to be free.

Then, instantly, it was gone.

The mirror was empty.

Daniel stared at his own face. For a moment he was still, and then he felt, deep within himself, something move. Something that fluttered and beat; with a gasp, he put both hands up to his chest in the darkness. Tiny tingles of restlessness surged in him; a fast heartbeat pulsing feverishly.

Rigid with shock, he stood looking at himself, the dark shadows of his eyes.

The bird was out.

The bird was in him.

✷✷✷

He slept, out of sheer weariness, but when he woke up he felt strange: light and restless, full of energy.

He made jerky, sudden movements, as if his co-ordination was gone; at breakfast he knocked a cereal bowl flying with his elbow, and the smash made his heart pound and flutter.

'What on earth's got into you?' his mother snapped.

He stared at her. 'What?'

'You. You're as jumpy as a cat.'

He looked round, uneasy. 'Nothing. Just a dream. At least, it might have been.'

His mother gave him a worried look. 'I hope you're not studying too hard.' She arranged Mrs Paulson's toast on a plate. 'You should get out with your friends more. How's Michael? Haven't seen him for ages.'

Daniel scowled. 'He's around.'

'Well, ask him here sometime. He seems a nice lad.' She turned. 'Take the tray up, will you? And *don't* drop it.'

Mrs Paulson always had breakfast in bed. When she had the tray comfortable and was unfolding the paper, she looked up at him. 'Well? Still lurking?'

He said, 'I just wanted to ask. That mirror – has it always been there?'

She put the paper down and stared at him. 'Whatever is it about the mirror?'

Seeing him shrug, she shook her head. 'Well, no, it hasn't. It was in the attic for years. The one at the end. I can't remember why now. I don't think George – that was my husband – cared for it very much. After he died, I had it brought down. Satisfied?'

He nodded. Inside him, the nerves of his fingers leapt and tingled.

The day passed in an intensity of sensation. Never had colour been so bright, never had the scents of flowers or the stink of chemicals in the lab been so pungent, so sharp. He felt restless and nervous, as if a great trapped energy struggled inside him. It was hard to settle, to concentrate on anything. Twice he saw Michael, once across a sea of faces in the canteen, but by the time he had pushed out of the queue and got over there, the table was empty.

Where was he?

What was he up to? The tingling in Daniel's chest rose to a panic; he forced it down, standing in the noisy hall with his hands clenched on the chair. After school. That would be the time. After school.

✱✱✱

On the bus, he knew it would be difficult. He wished he could get Michael on his own, away from the others, the sly, sneaky Hughes, and the rest of the gang with their big mouths and empty heads. They were all laughing at him now as he asked, 'Have you given them back?'

For answer, Michael took the keys out of his pocket and jangled them in Daniel's face. Daniel grabbed at them, but they were snatched away.

'What are you going to do?'

'Told you. Take a look inside.'

'Don't be stupid! What if she's there?'

'She's not.' Michael loosened his tie and took it off. 'She's got choir after school. Every Thursday.'

Tom James sneered. Daniel ignored him, feeling the power squirm in his chest. 'In that case, I'll stop you.'

'You!' Michael laughed. 'Go home, Dan. Do your homework. Stay out of this.'

Daniel stood up, but the bus turned a corner and juddered to a halt, and he swayed back into the seat. They were past him in seconds, off the bus, laughing, running up the street. Grabbing his bag, he pushed his way after them, jumping down as the bus was moving off, ignoring an angry yell from the driver.

He looked round. He didn't know where Mrs Lewis lived, or this village very well, at least not the back streets. Then he saw them, caught in the reflection of a window; they were behind him, running up a street of terraced cottages, noisy, fooling about. He ran after them.

Mrs Lewis' house turned out to be small and detached, set back from the road in an untidy garden. Purple crocuses sprouted by the door.

The gang stopped by the gate, crowding round.

'Spread out,' Tom snapped. 'Watch the street.' Then he turned and saw Daniel. For a moment, his face flickered with something like anger. 'What are you doing here?'

'I told you.' Daniel came up to him. 'What you're doing is stupid. It's not a joke. It's stupid. Give me the keys. I'll tell her I found them.'

Michael stared. 'She might not believe you.'

'It doesn't matter. She'll have them.'

Michael hesitated. Suddenly Daniel felt energy

shiver through himself. He grabbed Michael's arm. 'Listen, we used to be friends. Didn't we?'

Michael made no attempt to pull away. He gave a wry smile. 'So?'

'So we still are. Get rid of this lot. They only hang around you because they don't know what else to do. You're too good for them. You always were.'

'Me? I'm not even in the brains-band anymore.'

'Only because you've given up. If you worked…'

'Work!' Still smiling, Michael shook his head. 'Too late for that.'

'It isn't. Not for you, and you know it. You've got more intelligence than the rest of us put together…'

'…if only I'd use it. That's how it normally goes on. You sound like my mother.'

Daniel let go of him. They were both grinning.

Behind them, the gang was getting restless. 'If you've lost it,' Tom said abruptly, 'give us the keys. We'll do it.'

'You!' Michael turned around and looked him over coolly. 'You'd have trouble finding the keyhole.'

There was a cold silence. Then Tom moved up. 'Say that again.'

'Why should I? I'm not a parrot. And if you want the keys you'll have to come and take them.'

The hefty boy looked puzzled. 'Thought you had guts, Mike.'

'Maybe I have,' Michael said quietly. 'Maybe.'

The fight was sudden, and short. Tom punched hard, but Michael came back and shoved him fiercely into the hedge where he struggled, furious, among the privet. Daniel hauled him out and pushed him away and stood side by side with Michael, enjoying it. Hot and annoyed, Tom stared at them both in bewilderment. 'I don't get this. I thought you were with us.'

Michael shrugged. 'I thought I was too.'

'You'd better make up your mind.' Tom turned, marching off down the hill, the others after him. At the bottom of the road, they all laughed together, over-loud.

They turned the corner.

There was silence. A lorry droned past, up the lanes between the high hedges. Then Michael turned to him, curiously. 'What's got into you?'

Daniel grinned. 'You'd be surprised.'

They waited ages for another bus, talking about

131

ordinary things, Daniel jumping on and off the pavement restlessly. He didn't ask Michael home. They both knew he was coming. Finally, getting off the bus, he said, 'What about those keys?'

Michael shrugged, unconcerned. 'I'll put them back.'

'In her bag?'

'Why not? It'll be a laugh.' He stopped and faced Daniel, blocking the pavement. 'I would have gone in,' he said quietly.

Daniel nodded, gravely. 'I know you would. That's the trouble.'

His mother was out. He put his head round the door and said hello to Mrs Paulson, then they walked upstairs quickly, up towards Daniel's room, but he walked past it and down the dusty corridor to the closed attic at the end. Behind him, Michael said, 'Changed rooms?'

'No. I just want to have a look at something.'

The key was in the door. He turned it and went in. The attic was littered with boxes and chests and abandoned furniture. A stack of upturned chairs had legs jutting everywhere like a great spider in the dark. Paintings leaned against walls; Michael turned one round, then swung it up and looked at it, his hands black with dust. 'Might be worth a bit, this lot.'

'You can forget that idea for a start.' Daniel crossed to the window and looked down. On the sill, tiny and frail among the dust, were the bones of a bird. They lay scattered, disturbed by mice, the minute skull broken against the wooden frame.

He looked at then for a moment, then reached down and with all his strength wrenched up the stiff window, so that the cold air whirled in and whipped up a storm of dust.

'Hey!' Michael screwed up his eyes. 'Cut it out.'

Daniel didn't answer. He leaned both hands on the sill and looked out, breathing deep, letting it go, letting it leave him.

In the twilit garden the daffodils were pale ghosts. Far off in the trees, all the birds were singing.

NETTLE

7

She had two choices.

To hide here forever or to go home.

Even though it wouldn't be home for much longer.

Nia sat gloomily with her knees up in the brambles and bracken. It was safe enough, though she could hear the trains down on the line clattering and clanking by in the frosty air. A workman shouted somewhere. But he wouldn't come along here, would he?

The waste ground was a triangle of land between two railway lines and there was only a narrow path into it. The lines cut it off from the outside world. No one came here. It was her secret place.

The den had an earthen floor spread with an old piece of blanket that she kept dry by rolling it into a hole in the base of the hollow tree. It was completely woven over by brambles; now, in the winter cold, they were thorny and bare, but still thick enough to be a safe cover. Outside, snow had begun to fall, just a light dusting.

Nia picked at the fraying edges of the blanket and thought about the move.

It was all Lily's idea. Lily was Dad's partner; they had been together about a year. She had come to live with Nia and Dad and it had been fine at first, even though she had brought a lot of her own stuff that cluttered up the house, and her dog, Caspar, a really yappy little beast who annoyed the two cats. But it hadn't taken long before Lily had announced she wanted to move, and had made Dad want to move too. They'd even picked the house, a small, ugly, new one in an estate on the edge of town, all because Lily said the flat was too old and full of old fireplaces and dusty books and creaky corridors.

Which were exactly the things Nia liked best.

She scowled. She wanted to stay in her own room with the view of the trains. She liked to lie in the dark and listen to them, chuntering and rumbling away on mysterious journeys to strange places. Mostly they were freight trains, long, long chains of wagons with numbers stencilled on them, but sometimes there were passengers, and she would see a child waving or a woman reading, or a man fast asleep against the steamy window pane.

She liked imagining who they were and where they were going.

A few flakes of snow fell on her. She sighed and squirmed further back.

The shout came again.

She sat still, listening. All at once she realised it couldn't be a workman or a railwayman, because there were none on either line. She had checked before she had crawled into the den. And besides, it was such a strange, croaky shout.

Hoarse and angry.

It came from deeper in the bramble thicket, as if that could be possible, and it had sounded like *'Let me out! Let me out!'*

Nia breathed out an icy cloud. She forgot about being sad and got up on her hands and knees and peered in among the dead stems and earthen banks. Then she crawled deeper inside the brambles.

It was horrible. The spines snagged her hair and her coat, and she had to push her way through tangles of scratchy branches. Under her woolly gloves the soil was bare and cold, with worms wriggling deeper as she disturbed the deep litter of dead leaves that covered them. There were stones and bricks and she was worried there might be broken glass, but she kept on until finally she broke through into a tiny clearing and looked round.

Low brick walls, and piles of old wood.

Maybe there had been a building here once.

Some sort of signalman's hut or something?

The screech was coming from underneath the wooden planks, louder now.

'Let me out! Let me...'

'Hello?' she said quietly.

The voice stopped. She thought she heard a small gasp. Then, *'Who's that? Let me out! I'm trapped here! Please, let me out! Please help me!'*

It sounded so terrified she acted at once. She pulled the wooden planks away and pushed them aside. Underneath was a heap of earth. She tried to dig into it with her gloved hands, but that was no good, so she found a thin sharp piece of the wood and used that to pry and probe and scrape the earth away. When all the soil was clear, she found a large round grey stone. To her astonishment the voice was coming from underneath it.

'The stone! Roll the stone! It's so heavy on me! Quickly!'

She hesitated, but he sounded so desperate that she put the edge of the wood under the stone and pushed.

It was really heavy!

For a moment it didn't move at all, then it shifted just a little. She leaned harder, pushing with all her strength.

Suddenly the stone gave way. It tore up out of the soil, rolled a little way off and lay still.

Nia gasped, nearly falling after it.

She tossed away the piece of wood, and crouched down and stared into the hole.

There was a small wooden chest, made of some dark wood, with a rusty key in the lock.

'Turn the key!'

Nia hesitated again. Then she took hold of the key with her gloved fingers and wrenched it round.

She opened the lid.

141

Inside she saw the most amazing creature.

He was tiny. His face was wizened and old, but mostly what she could see was hair. Long yellow hair that tangled round and round him, like clothes. As if it had grown for centuries!

For a second, he lay quite still, looking up at her, blinking. He held up a tiny hand.

'Get me out.'

Nia took it, then gasped and snatched her hand away because even through the glove she had felt a sting on her fingers, sharp as acid.

The creature didn't care. He gave a great hoot of delight, scrambled up out of the chest, out of the hole and stood upright, breathing deep. Then he jumped and leapt and danced and kicked his heels. He whooped and screeched and yelled with savage delight.

Nia watched, eyes wide. She had to smile.

Finally, in mid dance, he stopped and turned and looked at her from one green eye. 'So,' he said, 'you've released me.'

'Yes.' Nia sat back on her heels, a little astonished. 'So I have. But how did you get in there?'

The tiny creature shrugged darkly. 'That doesn't matter.'

'What's your name?'

'Call me Nettle. And yours?'

'Nia.'

'Well, Nia, I am very grateful to you. Eternally grateful. You have no idea how grateful.' He danced and capered a few steps, until his hair tripped him. 'So now I must reward you. Say what you want. Anything. It's yours.'

'But…'

He held up a dirty hand. 'I don't usually do favours. And whatever you do, don't thank me. I HATE being thanked.'

'I…' She was a little scared of him. He was so sharp, so quick.

'Come on, hurry, hurry! What do you want?'

Her mind was a whirl. She had no idea what to say. So she said the first thing that came into her head. 'I want us not to move house.'

'Move a house! That's a huge spell…'

'No! NOT to move. My parents want us to live somewhere else.'

'And you don't want to?'

'NO! I want to stay where we are … I like it, and … it's my home.'

He shrugged as if he wasn't too interested. 'All right. NOT doing something is easy. Go home. It's fixed.'

'But … how?'

He scowled. 'I don't tell my secrets. Now I've paid you back, I'm off.' And just like that, with a twist up of his tangled hair, he was gone, scrambling and scratching through the brambles until all she could see were shaking branches.

Then there was nothing.

Nia shivered.

She realised she was freezing cold; it was snowing hard now. And she was scared.

Had all that really happened? She felt strange, and panicky; she fought her way out of the brambles back to the den, then raced down the path. It was already white with thin snow, and the clanking of the trains sounded louder and more ringing in the bitter air.

She ran all the way, under the wire fence, along by the rugby ground, through the subway under the road and up the lane to home. She had a strange dread that it would be gone, that all the world would be changed, but as she turned the corner of the street she took a great gasp of relief.

The house stood tall and reassuring at the end of its small row.

The windows of their flat were lit, and she could see the cat, Jess, sitting behind the curtains.

She ran in, pelted up the stairs and into the kitchen.

It was warm and empty. The TV was on in the next room; she slid out of her wet coat and boots quickly.

'Is that you, sweetheart?' Lily said.

'Yes.' She went into the kitchen, ready to be told off for being late, but at first glance she saw that wasn't going to happen.

Lily sat at the computer with the dog on her lap. She looked unhappy. Dad was frying bacon. He said, 'You're late.'

'Went for a walk.'

'In the snow?'

'Because of the snow!' She sat down at the table. There were some brochures from the estate agent lying there. She pushed them hurriedly aside, but

Lily sighed, put the dog down and closed the computer. She picked the brochures up and shoved them in a drawer. 'You don't have to worry,' she snapped. 'The move is off.'

Nia sat in absolute, astounded silence.

The sizzling of the bacon sounded louder than any sound she had ever heard.

'Don't you want to know why?' Lily asked. 'After all, I'm sure you're pleased.'

'Yes,' she whispered.

'Oh, it's nothing really,' Dad said hastily. 'The estate agent just rang and said the people who were going to sell their house to us have pulled out. No reason, they just seemed to have changed their minds. So we're back where we started.'

'We can stay here?' A great surge of delight rose inside her.

'For now. But…' He switched the gas off and turned, leaving the pan to go cold. He sat and took her hands across the table. 'You see, Nia, it's like this. We're going to need somewhere bigger than the flat soon. There's the three of us now, and the dog. And um … well … very soon, we'll be four.'

She stared at him, wide-eyed. 'Four?'

He smiled uncertainly. 'Yes. You will be having a little brother or sister. Lily is expecting a baby.'

It was as if the world exploded silently.

As if everything blew up in slow motion, like in a film.

She couldn't get her breath.

She couldn't think.

'We're so happy about it,' Lily said, though she sounded just a little nervous. 'I hope it's a girl, don't you? We'll all have such fun, Nia! And when she's born, and I can fit into a nice dress, maybe we'll get married. And you can be bridesmaid.' She smiled at Dad. 'Maybe.'

Nia put both her hands on the table and stared at them. 'That's great news,' she said.

And it was.

Dad gave her a hug. 'I knew you'd think so.'

She lay in bed that night and listened to the trains clanking by. There was one that came at exactly midnight. The midnight train, she called it. If she was awake, she always listened for it; it had a different, smoother sound, as if it ran on gold or silver wheels to mysterious lost countries where everyone was happy. Now, as she waited for it, she thought about the baby.

The baby would get all Lily's attention. That was right. She didn't mind about that.

But Dad would get all silly about it too. Maybe he'd go around with it strapped to his stomach and wheel it in the pushchair like modern dads were supposed to. Would the baby be more important than her? For a while, it would be. She knew that.

She rolled over. She didn't hate Lily. She wouldn't hate the baby. That would be mean and nasty. She didn't want to hate anybody! She just wanted her dad, and herself, just like it had always been, staying here, in their house.

The train came then, a silver-sweet rumble of sound. And, as she slipped into sleep, she dreamed she was on board it, and it was taking her deep into a tunnel of brambles. Brambles and thorns.

✳✳✳

'Hello!'

Nia bent under the thicket. 'Hello! Nettle! Are you here?'

She had been looking for half an hour and she was very cold. The afternoon was darkening already; the sky had that white, blank look that meant more snow. She hugged herself tight. 'Please come back. I need to speak to you. The spell … or whatever you did? I need you to do something more.'

Silence.

A rustle.

Then he said, 'I don't know why I should.'

He was sitting behind her, in the shadows of a broken fence. His hair looked more tangled than ever, his face small and unpleasant. She suddenly felt he was dangerous.

'I'm sorry. I mean, yes, it did work. We're not going to move just yet. The people selling changed their minds.'

He scowled. 'I know.'

'So…' She tried to concentrate, and not be scared. 'So that was good. But Lily's having a baby and they want a bigger place, but I still want to stay here. I don't know how you can fix that.'

He shrugged. 'There are ways. But why should I? I've done my bit for you. I've paid my debt. Unless of course, now you pay me.'

She stared. 'How?'

Nettle grinned. It was a sly, unpleasant grin; it scared her.

'You'll have to give me whatever I ask for.'

That seemed like a really bad bargain. She took a breath. 'Anything?'

'Anything.'

It was too much. But she so wanted to stay in their house! She shook her head. 'I can't.'

'Fine.' He folded his arms and squirmed round to turn his back on her. In the yellow tangle of thorns, he was almost invisible. 'You'll never see me again.'

'Wait!' She took a breath. 'I will give you anything you ask for, except – any of my family, my cats, my house, my books and my coral necklace. And nobody is to be hurt, not Dad, not Lily. Is that all right?'

He sniffed.

Was he disappointed?

But when he turned there was that sly grin again, and she hated it.

What had she done?

'It's a deal,' he said. 'Now go home.'

✱✱✱

When she came in at the front door, there was a strange silence.

The hall clock was striking five, and the radio was on somewhere. She put her foot on the stairs to go up to their flat, when a huge burst of laughter roared out from the door at the end of the passage,

Nia jumped.

That was where Mrs James lived, the old lady who owned the house.

The laughter was familiar. It was Dad's and Lily's.

Nia tiptoed down to the door. Just as she got there, it opened; Dad came hurtling out and nearly knocked her over.

'Here she is!' He grabbed her and pulled her in. 'Come and hear our wonderful news. You'll be so thrilled!'

She tumbled in. Mrs James' sitting room was large and spacious, with a big bow window that looked out onto the street. It was cluttered with dark Victorian furniture, big plants and a little electric fire that was always on and made the room stuffy.

On the table was a bottle of champagne, with tall glasses.

Lily put hers down guiltily. 'I shouldn't, you know.'

'But it's such a celebration.' Mrs James sat and patted the sofa next to her. 'Come and hear my news, Nia, lovely.'

She went and sat. She felt nervous.

'Now, then. I'm going to live with my daughter, in Cardiff. She has just got a new job, and wants me to be near her. Quite a few of my friends live there, and there is the theatre, and shops, so won't it be marvellous?'

'Yes,' Nia said, though she was sorry Mrs James was leaving. Mrs James always gave nice Christmas presents.

'And that's not all! Your father and Lily are going to buy the house from me. So the house will be yours! The whole house! What a lot of space you'll have!'

Nia stared, speechless. She couldn't believe what she was hearing. So it had worked! But how could Nettle have done this? An icy thread of terror crept into her.

Dad put a glass of champagne in her hand. 'You can have a sip. To celebrate. Just this once.'

She took a sip and it was sour and bubbly. She coughed.

They all laughed.

✱✱✱

That night, she waited for the midnight train. In the curled stillness, she thought about Nettle, out there, under the brambles. Was he waiting for her? Was he watching the house?

Finally, she got up and grabbed her dressing gown and padded to the window, looking out.

It was very cold.

The moon shone on the waste ground, glinted on the metal lines of the tracks. Snow fell softly, and the houses all down the road glimmered under its swirl.

Nia held her hands together tight.

She had a plan.

But she would have to be so careful!

As she thought it, the train hurtled out of the dark, and she gasped, because it was a rattling, fleeting vision of warmth and red seats, and faces. Window, window, window, flashing bright.

And then it was gone, and only the line hummed.

✦✦✦

'It doesn't make sense,' she said.

'It doesn't matter whether you think that or not.' Nettle stood small and tangled next to the rolled stone. He folded his arms across his yellow hair. 'I've done what you wanted.'

'You didn't do it! Mrs James and her daughter did it. They must have been planning it for a while. You didn't have time to do anything.'

He shrugged. 'Human time means nothing to me. Now. I want my reward.'

'But…'

'I want the baby.'

She gasped. 'WHAT! But I said … not my family!'

154

'It isn't born yet. So it's not your family, is it?' Sly and pleased with himself, he grinned at her. 'You promised, so you have to deliver. When it's born, you bring me the baby.'

Nia was appalled. She swallowed hard. Suddenly she knew she had to act now or this would all get so much worse. She said quickly, 'What you said about time…'

'Yes?'

'How long were you buried in that hole?'

'A thousand years.'

Amazed, she shook her head. 'I don't believe that.'

'It's true.'

'I think you were just hiding in that box. You had plenty of room. You just wanted to trick me.'

'No, no, NO!' He stamped his foot in fury. 'I was trapped!'

'You could have got out any time.'

'I could not!'

She shrugged, and bent and opened the chest. 'Show me, then…'

He jumped into it at once and curled up. 'See! It's tiny and I…'

Nia moved fast. She shoved the lid down and turned the key tight. Then she flung the chest in the hole in the ground. Furious shouting came out, but she ignored it, grabbing the stone and tugging it with all her strength until it rolled back heavily onto the lid of the chest and rested there. Pulling out the trowel she had brought, she piled the earth into the hole, more and more of it until it was a huge heap. Then she trampled it down. The cries from beneath were faint, not even words now. They sounded like the squeak of the snowy branches, the oily mutter of the trains.

Then she dragged the pieces of wood over and stood back, breathless.

Snow settled softly on the pile of rubbish.

There was nothing else there.

There had never been anything there.

What had come out was buried again.

✦✦✦

That night, as they ate supper, she asked a question she had never dared ask before. 'Dad, the trains on this line. Where do they actually go?'

'The city ... and then beyond. Down to the coast. To the sea.'

She nodded.

'Why?' he murmured softly.

'Because... Well...'

'And you don't seem as delighted about the house as I thought you'd be.'

She looked up. He was smiling, but he looked uncertain. Were they were doing this just for her?

'I am, but ... maybe I sort of think that we should move after all.' Now she knew they were staring at each other in astonishment over her head, and it made her smile. She dipped her spoon in her ice cream and licked it casually. 'Somewhere where the trains go. Somewhere by the sea.'

NOT SUCH A BAD THING

8

'I hope you're having a shower, Jack,' his mother said through the door.

'Yes.'

'And you will wear the new shirt and trousers?'

'Yes.'

'Mark says you can use some of his aftershave.'

'Fine,' he said wearily.

'And don't be too long! We can't have the winner turning up late.'

Jack heard her laughing all the way down the stairs.

He wasn't in the shower. He wasn't even undressed. He was sitting in his old jeans huddled up by the radiator, the big blue bath towel wrapped all round him. His head was under it, and it was dark in here, and warm, like a tent, and it felt safe. As if no one could get him here. As if the fear couldn't get him.

But the fear wasn't outside, he knew. It was in his belly, a cold lump. It made him sweat and shiver, and dried his mouth. Only six weeks ago it had been a tiny unease, easily laughed off, but day by day it had crept gradually into his sleep, into unguarded moments daydreaming in school, walking home, looking out of the window on the bus. He had tried not thinking about it but it had crept in. It had swollen and bloated, filling his fingers and eyes and throat. It was growing all the time. Soon it would choke him.

He flung off the towel and scrambled up, turned the shower on and let the water blast out hot. As he stood under it, he gasped at the stab of its needles on his skin.

It had been the homework that had started it – to write a story on any subject. Mr O'Driscoll's homework, and if it hadn't been him there would have been no problem. Because Jack had forgotten to do it, and with anyone else he could have asked for more time, come up with some excuse. But not to scary, scowling Mr O'Driscoll.

So he'd had the idea.

The stupid, stupid idea.

He'd gone into the front room and looked along the rows of Mark's books. Neither his mother or sister read much, but Mark had brought three shelves of books when he'd moved in – history mostly, but some fiction and a few books of short stories. One had caught Jack's eye; it looked old and battered, and the writers in it didn't have famous names he recognised like Shakespeare and Roald Dahl. He'd taken it to his room and flicked through. On page forty-six, he'd found something suitable. It was short and simple, only about five pages long. It didn't use fancy words. It was about a boy of twelve, just like him, and he'd never heard of the author.

Grinning, he'd reached for his laptop. Odds on, Mr O'Driscoll would never know.

Now, hurrying out of the shower, he dressed in the new trousers and scratchy shirt and dragged a comb through his hair. *Your sins will find you out.* That's what his nan always said. Was this what she meant?

The aftershave smelt too sweet; he put it back, then opened the steamed-up door and peered out.

Sarah charged out of her room past him. 'At last! I've been waiting *ages.*'

Jack shivered, cold again. He couldn't seem to keep warm.

He trailed downstairs and found Mark in his best suit reading the football results. 'Well, my son,' the big man said, looking him up and down, 'you look very smart.'

Normally that 'my son' would have angered Jack. Now he was too scared to care.

'Where's your mum?'

'Here.' She came in wearing the blue dress she'd worn for their wedding. Somehow that made it all worse.

The cat, Tom, was asleep on the table in the sun; when Jack smoothed him he rolled over and yawned, his belly soft and furry, his paws flopping ridiculously over his eyes. Rubbing the stripes, Jack wished he was a cat. Cats had no worries. Cats were never scared. He wanted to say he had a stomach ache, that he felt sick, that he couldn't possibly go. He clenched his fingers, took the breath to say it, but his mother turned him, looked him up and down, brushed the hair out of his eyes. 'I'm so proud,' she whispered.

When Sarah was ready, they trooped out to the car. Mrs McGuire next door had come out.

'Big day then?'

His mother nodded. She looked young and was wearing red lipstick. 'It's two o'clock at the Middleton Hotel. A buffet and everything.'

Mrs McGuire smiled her wrinkly smile at Jack. 'And what's the prize?'

'A hundred pounds.' The words were ashes in his mouth.

She opened her eyes wide, the way people do to show kids they were surprised, but before she could say anything else, he turned and scrambled into the car. He couldn't bear anything else.

The car smelt of perfume and warm leather. Jack stared out of the window, grimly.

Of course, Mr O'Driscoll hadn't recognised the story. The mark had been A*.

A very striking piece of work, Mr O'Driscoll had scrawled in the margin. *Well done!*

Everything would have been all right if Mrs Harris hadn't seen it.

As the car droned up the hill and round the roundabout, Jack wondered how things happen, how they lead to each other. Because that had been the stroke of fate, the terrible blow.

She was blonde and enthusiastic and the Head of English. She'd come up to him in the corridor at the end of one break time and said, 'Jack, I want a word.'

They'd gone into an empty classroom, out of the noise, and his heart had sunk, but she'd turned and smiled at him brightly, her glasses catching the sun.

'That story you wrote. Mr O'Driscoll showed it to me and it's excellent, Jack, really.'

He mumbled something.

'So I hope you won't mind, but I've entered it.'

'Entered it?'

'Into the competition in Cardiff. Children's Short Story category. You don't mind?'

Jack had shaken his head and walked out, dazed. Looking back, it was then that the fear had started, the disbelief. Because she hadn't found him out either. He had wanted to tell her, but it would have been embarrassing. And besides, the story would come nowhere. The judges would spot it.

The car stopped.

He looked up and saw the hotel, the new one, its entrance hall lit with chandeliers. His mother said,

'How grand!' and giggled, and Sarah gave herself an extra quick spray of perfume.

He got out, because there was nothing else to do now. Climbing the marble steps he heard again the drop of the letter through the letterbox, his mother running up the stairs with it to his bedroom, saw the wide, heavy cream envelope with his name on the printed label.

Dear Jack, it had said. ***I am delighted to be able to inform you that your story*** – the title had been written in blue biro – ***has been awarded First Prize in the 12-14 age group…***

*** * *** * ***

'This way.' His mother turned through wide double doors into the room. Behind her, Jack stared in dismay.

The room was full.

The audience wasn't all children either, but a lot of adults, a few reporters, the mayor, some arty-looking men and women up at the table in the front who must be the adjudicators. Jack's hand was limply shaken, a badge was pinned on him, he and Mum and Sarah and Mark were led in a hot embarrassed progress up the central aisle to front row seats with RESERVED cards on. He sat down. Against the back of the chair, his shirt stuck to him; sweat prickled his upper lip.

It took an age for the event to start, but when it did things were worse. The adjudicator for his event was a tall, stern man in a dark velvet jacket; he talked about *plot* and *character* and the *vivid resonances of the juvenile imagination* and Jack almost slipped into boredom until the voice jerked him upright by talking about his story, its clever imagery, its freshness, its innocence.

Every word was a torment. He watched the man in fixed horror, trying to shut out the sounds, hating him, furious with him, because he stood up there like someone important, spouting as if he knew it all, but he didn't, did he? *He had no idea.* Were all adults such frauds, was it all false, the way they pretended to know things, to be experienced, to have learned, have passed exams? Were they really all fakes like he, Jack, was?

Mum tapped his knee. Maybe he was fidgeting,

maybe she was just happy. And the judge was looking at him and saying, 'And now the winners will read their prize-winning work.'

For a moment, it was too shocking to sink in.

Read it!

Here!

In front of them all!

He froze in his seat, his spine icy. His heart thudded painfully in his chest.

It was all happening too quickly. The boy in third place was tall, and second place went to a dark-haired girl, and they got up and read, the boy in a whisper and the girl in a firm, confident voice, but he didn't understand a word. It was a buzz and jumble of sound. All there was left to do was watch their lips, his hands knotted tight, his entire being shrunken to a shrivelled tiny lump of terror somewhere inside him.

Waiting.

Just waiting.

When they called his name his heart gave a shuddering thump. Somehow he stood up.

The papers were put in his hand; he was shaking, but he was guided kindly to a stand and

169

he slid them on there and took a breath. Then he looked up over the rows of faces.

And saw Dad.

Dad was at the back. He was just inside the door, by a woman taking photographs. He grinned and put his thumb up and Jack stared back, rigid.

Nan must have told him. Mum wouldn't have.

He licked his lips. He wanted to whisper into the microphone that there had been a mistake, that it wasn't his fault, that he hadn't deserved all this misery. He wanted to explain that Mum had started to take an interest in his homework now, that Sarah wasn't so sarcastic. That a hundred pounds would go towards a new laptop and that wasn't such a bad thing to want, was it? He wanted to tell them that Mark was arrogant and Dad looked so lost, down there on his own, so far away. And that the fear had grown around him and closed like a trap and there was no way out and he couldn't bear to think of Mum's face if she found out.

He wanted to yell at them that it was all their fault.

Instead, there was only the story.

170

The story waited for him, inevitable. He looked at the reporter and photographer and finally understood that the story would be printed in tomorrow's newspaper. Someone was sure to recognise it, and ring in.

They couldn't all be this stupid.

The money would be taken away and the second-place girl would get it and everyone would know. There would be humiliation and rows. Mockery in school.

Jack rubbed his nose, and looked out at the world, at his mother's happy smile.

'This is my story,' he said quietly. 'It's called *Not Such a Bad Thing.*'

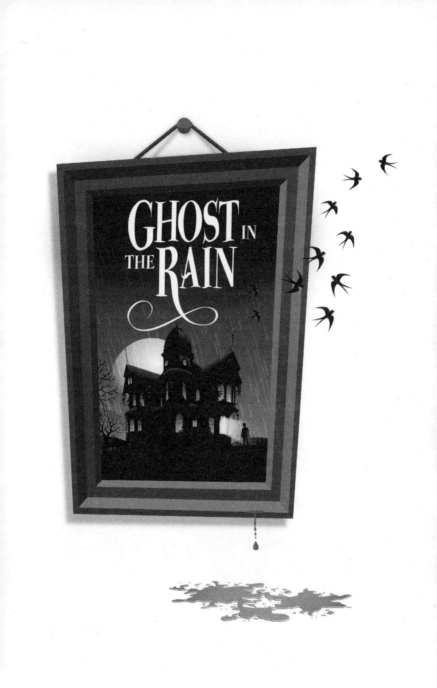

GHOST IN THE RAIN

9

Every year, since I was eight, I've come to stay at Maes-y-Rhiw for the summer. It is a long journey, especially as I have to travel on my own, but the first glimpse of the old red-brick house on its knoll, with the lake reflecting it like a mirror, always gives me a warm, safe, happy feeling.

I remember the first time I came. That time it was by train. I stood outside the station, pressed into the hedge as the carts and cattle crowded by to the market at Trenewydd. My bag was very heavy; I put it down in the dust and looked hopefully up the lane at the small dog-cart rattling towards me, its pony trotting between the high hedges. When it pulled up, a dark-haired woman in a grey habit was looking down at me.

'You must be Sarah?'

I nodded nervously. 'That's right.'

'I'm your Aunt Alicia. Don't look so scared, girl, I won't eat you. Is that your bag?' She had it on the seat next to her already; she moved very quickly and abruptly, just as she spoke. 'In you get.'

Climbing up, I saw her glance over me critically, my frock, stockings, shoes and new blue coat. Then she flicked the pony into a walk. 'You're very neat. How old are you?'

'Eight, Aunt.'

'Can you dress yourself, and all that?'

I looked at her in surprise, and she caught my eye. 'Well, good,' she said, with a laugh. 'I've no nanny or nurse at Maes-y-Rhiw. Mrs Powell is the cook, but she's got no time to fuss and fidget over a great girl like you. And I have my work. I'm afraid you'll have to amuse yourself for much of the time. Try not to get into scrapes, won't you?'

My mother had warned me about this. Aunt Alicia was an artist; she painted landscapes and portraits and even had them shown in big exhibitions in London and Cardiff. I like to paint and draw too. My tutor, Mr Waterhouse, had even said to my mother that I had talent, and safe in my bag, packed flat among my nightdresses, were two of my best sketches that I had brought for my aunt to see. I remember how I rubbed the seams of my new white gloves, and wondered if I would dare show them.

Then we turned a corner, and there was the house, with red creeper smothering the brickwork, and the house martins and swifts skimming in the hot sky.

Well, I was right. I never did get to show her those drawings. I soon found out that my mother had warned me well; Aunt Alicia had no time for me, no time for anything except her work. I only saw her at mealtimes, and sometimes not even then, for if it was fine Mrs Powell would let me take bread and cheese and an apple into the garden and eat there, swinging in the pliant cedar branches. It was Mrs Powell who looked after me, as far as anyone did, but most of the time I was free to wander where I wanted; I could have left the grounds and walked for miles over the fields, and no one would even have noticed.

But it was the garden that I loved, and I still do. Every time I come here, I spend most of my time out there. This year, as always, I've come back in the height of summer, when the afternoons are long and hot, and the butterflies dance in the heated borders, in a haze of phlox and delphinium.

The part of the garden I like best is the small walled plot to the south of the house. A high brick wall shelters it; trees and shrubs make it shady and secret. I've always had it to myself – Aunt Alicia never goes in. But this year, someone else was there.

I saw him first on the night I arrived.

The room I always have is on the corner of the house: a small room with pink wallpaper and heavy dark furniture. I was sitting on a cushion on the windowsill, looking down. It was about nine o'clock in the evening. The great cedar that grew by the wall was a black mass, rustling faintly. Beyond it the garden lay in shadow, a whisper of scents and stirrings. An owl flew over the wall and away to the wood beyond. The night was so still that I could hear the horses in the stable, shuffling their straw.

It was then I saw him.

He looked about thirteen.

He stepped out from the bushes onto the grass, almost below my window, so that the light from the drawing room lit the side of his face and his

178

fair hair. For a moment, I thought he was peeping in at Aunt Alicia; then he turned and ran over the lawn, silently.

In the corner where the trees grew thick and dark, there was an old well. No one used it. A low stone coping had been built around it years ago and the shaft was closed with a wooden lid, green now and half rotten. It was a dank, unlucky place.

I watched as the boy walked around the well, looking down. Once he turned a pale face to the house, and then paused, resting both hands on the stone brim. He wore a white shirt that glimmered against the branches.

I stood up, suddenly uneasy.

The boy lifted the edge of the cover; he slid it back slowly, as if it was heavy, and leaned over and looked down. I imagined the darkness down there, the horrible stagnant smell, the slimy walls. Perhaps he was trying to see his reflection, or had dropped something, because now he was leaning right over, leaning too far, and a thread of fear squirmed in me. I gripped the window frame.

'Be careful!' I hissed. 'You'll fall!'

His head jerked up. I saw him stare at the house,

his eyes moving along the line of windows. I turned, ran out into the corridor and down the long stair to the hall. The garden door was ajar; I slipped through, round the side of the house and under the rose-arch.

The garden was empty.

Very slowly, I walked across the lawn to the well. The cover lay to one side. I looked down. There was nothing but darkness, and a smell – as I had thought, a bitter tang of decay. Knee-deep in the long grass, I looked around.

Behind me, only one line of footprints marked the dew on the lawn.

✱✱✱

After breakfast next morning, Aunt Alicia went out. From the morning room, I watched her climb into her carriage. She looked older this year; her hair was quite grey now, and she moved slowly, like someone with a secret sorrow. I had noticed it come on her two years ago, this sudden ageing.

When the carriage had gone, I went out into the

garden and spent the morning swinging in the cedar tree. I was quite used to being by myself, but I wondered a great deal about the boy.

Who was he, and what had interested him so much about the well?

Below me, waist-deep in the lavender and roses, Siôn, the old man who looked after the garden, leaned on his fork. He was talking to his grandson, the farm boy who brought the eggs. I saw them glance towards the well and, suddenly curious, I slid down a little, making sure they didn't see me.

'...almost three years ago,' the old man was saying.

'I remember, *Taid*. I was here, that night.'

'And it's changed her. She blames herself. Thinks if she'd had more time for the child, see? But she was always busy. There, it happened, Ben. It can't be undone.'

Ben nodded, scratching his ear. 'And what you said in the Red Lion, about...'

'Now, don't go repeating what I said in the Lion, boy, or I'll lose this situation and never get another, not at my age. There's no call for gossip.' Siôn ran a finger round inside his dirty collar. 'Still, it's true, for all that. There's times now, when I'm working here alone, maybe in the afternoon, or after tea, when I know someone is watching me. Someone silent. And it's worse by that well.'

'It would be,' Ben said, his eyes wide.

'And I'll tell you something else. If I've nailed that well cover down once, I've nailed it twenty times. But if you went over there now, you could lift it, easy as easy. The nails just disappear.' He shook his head. 'The night they brought that poor little mite's body up, I knew how it would be.'

He stopped then, and perhaps he'd heard me, because soon after they moved away, round the side of the house.

I sat there, quite still. So old Siôn thought that the garden was haunted. And it was true. I knew it was true. After a moment, I climbed down, getting green smears from the bark on my hands and dress, and dropped lightly into the grass.

The well was dark, as always. Trees hung over it, and ivy swarmed up the sides. No sunlight ever came here; the grass was still wet, and snails, colonies of them, were clustered on the stones. The old man had been right about the cover; I slid it aside easily.

Looking down, there was my face, small and white in the black ring of the water, and behind me the green branches, filling the sky.

Then I turned quickly.

The boy was leaning against a tree, a few yards away. He wore the same clothes as before, and his face was pale and narrow. He was watching me intently.

'Hello,' I said.

'Hello.' He straightened and came forward, stopping just out of touching distance. 'Who are you?'

'Sarah. Aren't you a bit cold, with no coat?'

He shrugged. 'Not really.'

I wondered whether to say that I had seen him the night before, but decided not to. He came up to the well and put his hands among the ivy and looked over.

'I think someone once drowned here,' I said slowly, dragging the hair from my cheek. The wind moved the branches above us; spots of rain pattered on the leaves.

'Drowned?' The boy looked at me, and moved closer. His hands were thin, the fingers dirty with broken nails. 'Imagine, falling down there.' Together, we looked down. 'Imagine it,' he muttered. 'You'd kick and struggle and scream and no one would come, and then you'd go under, in the black water, and under again…'

I shuddered. 'You didn't tell me your name.'

'Huw Meredith. I'm staying here.'

I stared at him. 'Are you?'

'Yes.' He came closer, put out a hand. I forced myself to stand still, but as his fingers came closer to my sleeve, he said, 'You shouldn't be afraid. Not of the well…'

'Child! Come away from there!'

We both turned. Mrs Powell was standing at the drawing-room window, her dress and shawl flapping. 'Come here!' she said angrily.

I looked at the boy.

'Tonight,' he said. 'I'll wait for you here. At ten.'

All afternoon it rained, beating the flowers flat and rolling from the leaves into the soaking grass. The lake was a darkness between the trees, its surface dimpled with rain, and from all the downstairs windows in turn, I watched the drops slide and patter down the glass. Even after tea, when the sky darkened and the wind dropped, even then the rain fell, in light taps and trickles of sound outside the house.

I waited until I heard Mrs Powell serve my aunt's supper. Then I opened the door of my bedroom and slipped out. The corridor was gloomy, its ends invisible. The great staircase curved down into the dimness, and peering through its twisted bannisters I could see one candle burning down there, on the sideboard by the mirror.

I came down, silently.

The only sound was the clock, its deep *tock* and the soft click and stir of the invisible pendulum.

Halfway along the hall, a slot of red, flickering light fell across the darkness; the drawing-room door was open. Hidden in the heavy purple folds of curtain, I looked in and saw Aunt Alicia sitting on the sofa before the fire. She did not see me. Her hair was untidy; wisps of it hung down and she wound them absently around her fingers. The room was littered with unfinished paintings and sketches were piled on the tables. She looked as people do sometimes when they don't know they are being watched, tired and unguarded, her back straight and her gaze hard and empty.

I tiptoed across the doorway and ran down the kitchen passage to the garden door. It was ajar again. Rain was pattering into a pool on the doorstep, but when I stepped outside and looked up, the cloud was broken and ragged, with dark patches of sky glinting with stars. Between the bushes the ground was muddy; water drops fell in showers from the springy branches.

The boy was waiting by the well; he was sitting on the edge, his shirt a glimmer in the darkness. He stood up as I crossed the lawn, and smiled.

'I knew that you'd come.'

'I said I would.' Carefully, I sat on the wet stone. 'You've opened the well.'

'It's easy to open.' He stepped closer, looking down. 'I always come here.'

'Why?'

He gave me a strange, sidelong glance. 'Do you know what I think? I think there are countries down there somewhere; that if you climb down far enough, you might come to a place with castles and where the animals can talk, and where ogres are. Don't you think so? Like the stories where the youngest son always comes off best.'

'I don't know,' I said doubtfully. 'Perhaps.'

'I wish there were.' He scowled down at his reflection. 'I used to be a youngest son.'

'Used to be?'

He stood up, quickly. 'I hate it here. It's so old and so dull and no one speaks to you and there's nothing to do. I've wanted to go home for ages, but I can't. Not yet. It will be different now, though, now you've come.' He looked at me eagerly. 'I'll have someone to play with, someone to talk to. Do you climb trees?'

'All the time.'

The wind moved the branches around us, spattering raindrops down the well. Our far-deep reflections rippled and blurred.

'And there's no need to be afraid of ghosts,' he said suddenly, 'is there?'

187

'I don't think so,' I said. 'I'll come tomorrow, if you like.'

'Promise?'

'Promise.'

And I smiled at him, and let myself disappear very slowly, so as not to alarm him.